DOGBOY

DOGBOY

CHRISTOPHER RUSSELL

GREENWILLOW BOOKS
An Imprint of HarperCollins*Publishers*

This book is a work of fiction. References to real people, events, establishments, organizations, or locales are intended only to provide a sense of authenticity, and are used to advance the fictional narrative. All other characters, and all incidents and dialogue, are drawn from the author's imagination and are not to be construed as real.

Dogboy
Copyright © 2006 by Christopher Russell
First published in 2005 in Great Britain
by Puffin Books as *Brind*.
First published in 2006 in the United States by
Greenwillow Books.

The right of Christopher Russell to be identified as the author of this work has been asserted by him.

The text of this book is set in Cochin.
Book design by Chad W. Beckerman

Library of Congress Cataloging-in-Publication Data
Russell, Christopher
Brind / by Christopher Russell.
p. cm.
"Greenwillow Books."
Summary: In 1346, twelve-year-old Brind, an orphaned kennel boy raised with hunting dogs at an English manor, accompanies his master, along with half of the manor's prized mastiffs, to France, where he must fend for himself when both his master and the dogs are lost at the decisive battle at Crécy.
ISBN-10: 0-06-084116-8 (trade bdg.)
ISBN-13: 978-0-06-084116-4 (trade bdg.)
ISBN-10: 0-06-084117-6 (lib. bdg.)
ISBN-13: 978-0-06-084117-1 (lib. bdg.)
[1. Knights and knighthood—Fiction. 2. Orphans—Fiction. 3. Mastiff—Fiction. 4. Dogs—Fiction. 5. Human-animal relationships—Fiction. 6. Crécy, Battle of, Crécy-en-Ponthieu, France, 1346—Fiction. 7. Hundred Years' War, 1339-1453—Fiction] I. Title.
PZ7.R9153854Dog 2006 [Fic]—dc22 2005008525

First American Edition 10 9 8 7 6 5 4 3 2 1

 GREENWILLOW BOOKS

This book is dedicated to Christine,
who has all my best ideas

CONTENTS

DOGBOY

I

BRIND

The dogs were getting closer. The boy could hear their music. Deep-throated, eighty voices together, calling as one now that they were locked on to the scent. His scent. He ran on. Low-growing hazel branches lashed his face. Brambles tore and snatched at his legs. Tree roots, hidden in the leaf mold, tried to trip and bring him down. Over a fallen oak, its dead wood cracking in his hands as he grabbed and clambered. Then the stream, ice cold and slippery under his bare feet. He paused in the mud on the far side. Where now? His heart seemed to fill his whole body and head with its thumping. The stream tinkled unconcernedly. The boy wanted to lie down and roll in it, to splash and cool his hot face, but there was no time. He had to run.

The stream caused the dogs no confusion. The boy's scent was strong and fresh. Very fresh. The pack leader spoke and plunged across and the others followed, taking up the call again, excited, expectant. Born to hunt.

The boy was running uphill now. Fewer trees, firmer ground, but it was steep and getting steeper. The muscles in his legs began to stiffen, his knees shrieked at him to stop, but he couldn't, not yet. Not yet. Then the ground leveled unexpectedly and straight ahead of him was a cliff of chalk. He'd gone wrong. There shouldn't be a cliff, just a path through low-growing blackthorn up onto the downs. Confused, he cast around, then stumbled on toward the cliff, as if the path would suddenly appear. But there was only the cliff, high and wide and sheer. The hound music was momentarily quieter, deflected by the change in level of the ground, but the boy knew the dogs were still coming.

He tried to climb the cliff, clutching at tufts of grass and deep-rooted blackthorn, clawing his way upward. But the chalk was treacherous, crumbling beneath his toes and coming away in his fingers, so that he slipped and fell, scraping and bloodying his knees as he went. And as he hit the ground, the dogs arrived. The boy picked himself up and faced them. There was nowhere to run, and he could run no further anyway. The chase was over.

The dogs crowded forward triumphantly behind the pack leader, their noise deafening now that they were so close. Mastiffs. Massive and powerful. Born to hunt and trained to kill. The pack leader launched itself at the boy, knocking him to the ground and pinning him there with huge, hard paws. The boy felt a gust of suffocating dog's breath as the mastiff opened jaws that could snap a man's neck.

And then it licked him. A slobbering lick from chin to forehead. The helpless boy gurgled with pleasure as the dog lapped at his nose, his cheeks, his ears, while its tail wagged furiously. The boy grabbed the dog's own ears and waggled them, then was aware of yelping and turmoil, and the crack of a whip.

The rest of the pack was backing off, turning and cowering. The whip cracked again, inches from the boy's head and that of the pack leader. Voices shouted, men's voices, one harsher and closer than the rest. The pack leader sprang sideways from the boy as the whip bit into its flank. And the boy found himself staring up at a man on a sweating horse. The man seemed very high above him. High as the blue sky itself.

"Get up, you little cur," the man said.

The boy did as he was told.

"Good chase, Tullo," he panted.

The man grunted. "Better still if they'd torn you to bits."

He turned his horse away and cracked the whip again at the mastiffs. Men on foot were using sticks, herding the dogs into a dense, subdued mass. The leader of the pack glowered and snarled at the man on the horse but backed slowly into the pack, no longer the dominant leader but a wary, resentful subject, acknowledging the power of the whip.

Then they were gone. Men, dogs, and horses. Out of sight, back down the hill toward the stream, the forest, and home. Leaving the boy where he stood, as if he were nothing to them. Which he was. Except to the dogs.

Sir Edmund Dowe was a happy man. He watched with pride as the pack of mastiffs, his mastiffs, the finest in all of England, streamed back into their paddocks. He leaned on the wooden rail, Tullo, his huntsman, standing beside him.

"They're looking fit, Tullo. Plenty of muscle. And they did well this morning."

"Well enough, sir, but the boy was lazy. Should have run farther."

Sir Edmund frowned. "Cain's Cliff, you said. That's more than far enough."

"He'll ruin them." Tullo's voice was bitter.

"Far enough for the hounds." Sir Edmund gave the sour-faced man a hard look. "And for me."

Tullo nodded curtly. "Sir."

There was resentment rather than agreement in his eyes. But he knew who was master, just like the hounds.

"Kempe has a dead cow," said Sir Edmund. "Take the cart and fetch it for their supper."

He returned his gaze to the mastiffs, dismissing Tullo, who nodded again. "Sir," he said, and walked away.

Sir Edmund didn't like the man, didn't like him at all. But he was a good huntsman. Over-generous in his use of the whip, perhaps. And the chain. And the stick. But dogs, like servants, had to be taught to mind their manners. Tullo knew his countryside and was cunning in the ways of deer, hare, and boar. That was all one wanted of a hunts-man. He didn't need to be likeable. And he did keep the kennels in splendid order. Sir Edmund was almost as proud of his kennels as he was of the mastiffs who lived in them. Like the mastiffs themselves, the kennels were the finest in England, without doubt. Sir Edmund had designed them himself. There was accommodation for forty males and forty bitches, kept in two separate blocks, each with its own exercise paddock, feeding yard, and sleeping lodge.

Sir Edmund's wife said he spent more time, trouble, and money on his dogs than he did on her, which was true. But then, it was a wife's place to come a poor third behind fighting and hunting. Sir Edmund was fond of his wife, of course. He wouldn't have married her otherwise. He had been sixteen and she fifteen and he had won her favor at a tournament. It had been the only occasion ever when he had managed to knock an opponent off a horse. He had been lucky and sweet young Beatrice had been impressed. Or had seemed to be. But that was a long time ago now. They had no children, which must be Beatrice's fault, but it didn't really matter; he still had his armor. And his dogs.

Sir Edmund turned to watch Tullo stalking out of the yard with Hatton, the carter. As they went, the kennel boy, Brind, came running in past them. He looked exhausted and his feet and legs were bleeding after the morning's chase. Tullo helped him on his way with a swipe from his coiled whip. The boy fell respectfully at Sir Edmund's feet, crouching in his doglike way before barking out his news.

"Horseman coming!"

Tullo hacked at the carcass with the cleaver. He had already skinned the dead cow with his hunting knife and now he attacked it with methodical venom, as if he hated it. This shouldn't be his job. He was the huntsman, not a kitchen skivvy. But the kennel cook was ill with a fever. Again. Time *he* was put in the pot with the other useless carcasses. The cleaver splintered bone and Tullo felt a little better.

Through the thin wall of the cooking hut he could hear the mastiffs in their paddocks and Brind talking softly to them. The little cur. Out there checking the hounds for injury after the morning run. What did he know? He was no better than a dog himself and should be treated as such. Yet day by day he wheedled himself deeper into Sir Edmund's affections. Burrowing like a tick.

Tullo brought the cleaver down so hard that it stuck fast in the chopping block. He heaved it free. Sir Edmund was a fool. But Tullo wasn't. That horseman. He'd still been at the manor when Tullo had returned with the dead, stinking cow, and he was still here now. Nobody knew what was going on. But Tullo had spotted the rider's livery when the great horse had thundered past in the lane earlier, spattering Hatton and himself with mud. Golden leopards on a red field. He was from the king.

It was Brind's favorite place. He loved the warmth. The dark. The smell of dog and bracken. Always clean bracken. Brind made sure of that. Every evening, while the hounds were outside, waiting to be fed, Brind changed the bracken in the sleeping lodges, spreading armfuls of fresh, sweet fern along the low wooden benches on which the mastiffs slept. On which Brind slept, too. As he'd always done, since soon after he'd been found among a litter of mongrel pups twelve summers ago. He'd been bigger than the other blind, mewling newborns, but the mother hadn't seemed to notice. She was licking him clean just like she was the others when Milda, the kitchen girl, came into the old stable, looking for eggs. Brind had lived with dogs ever since. It had seemed natural. And Sir Edmund, who owned him and all the dogs on the manor, had seen no reason to change that.

Brind understood that he wasn't a dog, but he had no recollection of a human mother. Nor a father, for that matter. He must have had both: Everything had a mother and a father. But it didn't trouble him. His mother probably died in birthing. Human mothers often did. If not the mother, then the human whelp often died. Brind wondered why humans produced only one whelp at a time. He'd seen pregnant women on the manor farm. How heavy they became and for so many moons. And then to birth only one whelp, which often died. Dog mothers had litters of at least six. Even if one or two died, there were still plenty left. It made much more sense. Brind listened to Tullo shouting in the feed yard. He always shouted at the hounds. And shouted at Brind for not shouting at them. Brind didn't need to shout, but Brind didn't understand humans like he understood dogs. He circled on the deep bracken, making himself a comfortable nest, claiming his spot before the mastiffs came jostling in after their supper. And very soon he was asleep, dreaming of rolling in clear, cool streams.

Sir Edmund stared at his wife as if she had just suggested that the world was round.

"Not go?" he said. "Not *go*!"

"Don't shout at me, dear."

Lady Beatrice was being reasonable. Sir Edmund always felt at a disadvantage when his wife was reasonable. It was like trying to push water uphill.

"But I'm a knight!"

"Yes, dear."

"Summoned by my liege lord, the king."

"Yes, dear."

"The king, Beatrice. We are at war with France!"

"We are always at war with France. If you go, you will be seasick. You were the last time."

"I am a knight, woman! I live to fight for my king. That is the purpose of my existence!"

"No, it isn't."

Pushing water uphill.

"The purpose of your existence is to care for your own people, here on your own land, to provide them with food and shelter, not go trampling across France, destroying the food and shelter of others."

"It is not a matter of trampling, it is a matter of honor. Of chivalry! Of killing Frenchmen."

"Your grandfather was a Frenchman."

That was true.

"And so was mine."

Also true.

"We speak French. We make our servants speak French."

Yes, yes. French was still the official language of England; it had been since the time of the Conqueror. That was not Sir Edmund's fault. And she was right about the seasickness. But he was a knight. He would fight on.

"Supposing every knight in the realm refused the call to arms? What would the king do then? Other than cut off all our heads as traitors?"

"There are plenty enough who will go and take pleasure in it. And plenty enough who will do it for money. Especially the archers. The king needs archers more than he needs elderly knights in rusty armor."

Elderly! Sir Edmund was on his feet.

"If I am elderly, madam, then so are you!"

It was ungallant but she had gone too far. His wife merely shrugged.

"I am just forty years old, Beatrice, and never fitter."

He held in his stomach, preempting another unkind truth.

"And I *will* fight for my king!"

He stumped out and slammed the great oak door satisfyingly behind him. But a few seconds later he was back.

"Do you have the key to my war chest?"

She was standing at the window and didn't turn to him as she replied.

"It is by the hearth, where it always is."

Sir Edmund grunted, angry with himself for not remembering, and went to the hearth, where he took the blackened key from its hook, then paused at the door on his way out again. He didn't like his wife arguing with him, but he felt more uneasy with her silence.

"Who will you take with you?" she asked, still with her back to him.

Silence would have been better, after all. The king's messenger clearly expected a retinue, and actually had written down that Sir Edmund would bring twenty men-at-arms to the war host. Sir Edmund had got rather carried away by then. Perhaps it was the second flagon of wine they'd shared. Good French wine. He didn't have twenty men. Or even ten.

"Philip, of course."

Philip was his nephew and page. Aged thirteen.

"Hatton . . ." He paused a beat to make it sound inconsequential. "And Tullo."

Lady Beatrice turned.

"Tullo?"

Sir Edmund shrugged. "I shall take the hounds. If the campaign is long, we shall need some sport. And to hunt meat."

He didn't tell her the whole truth. He couldn't face another assault of reason.

"So poor little Brind will go too?"

"Naturally."

He was beginning to feel in control again but, after another brief silence, Lady Beatrice looked straight at him.

"I would prefer you here and alive, Edmund."

Her voice was quiet, dignified. It was the point of no return. Sir Edmund couldn't find a suitable answer. He looked at the floor, held the key tight in his fist, and left the hall.

War chest was a rather grand name for the long box of darkened oak with its rusty hinges and dry rot in one corner, but it contained Sir Edmund's other pride and joy besides his hounds: his armor. And it was *not* rusty. Well, it wouldn't be once Philip had been set to burnish it. Sir Edmund knelt before the chest and lifted out the pieces one by one.

It was, in truth, a mixed lot. Old-fashioned chain mail and a few small bits of the more modern plate metal. Wealthy knights nowadays paid a fortune for complete sets of plate and covered their horses with the stuff as well. Sir Edmund wasn't wealthy. Eight years ago, before his last campaign, and at his wife's insistence, he had bought a closed helm, complete with visor, to protect his head, but that was it. Besides, he still had his trusty shield.

He stood up and lifted it down from the wall. The weight of it made him gasp, but he was sure he would soon get used to carrying it again. He gazed at the coat of arms painted on its leather cover. *His* coat of arms. Three black hounds on a green field. The hounds were more gray than black now and the green field also had faded; but Sir Edmund's eyes and the back of his neck still prickled at the sight.

With a surge of warlike emotion, he pulled his great broadsword down from the wall. It refused to budge from its scabbard but he swung it exultantly around the chamber anyway, swishing it two-handed at the walls and furniture and finishing with a fatal stab at the lid of the war chest. It took him more than a minute to recover his breath. Then he remembered the other key. His secret key.

He knelt down again and delved at the bottom of the war chest, feeling for the small leather bag hidden beneath the jumble of gauntlets and sword belts. As he found it, somebody knocked on the chamber door. Sir Edmund scrambled to his feet.

"Who is it?"

"Philip, sir."

The voice was feeble and high. Sir Edmund was certain he himself had been more grown-up at thirteen. He slipped the leather bag inside his tunic.

"Come in, dear boy."

Brind lay snuggled in the predawn dark. Against his head, a hound's warm flank gently rose and fell. Against his curled back, another's head pressed heavy in sleep. Further along the bench a dog spoke in its dreams, then twitched violently, provoking a snarl from its neighbor before half waking, burrowing deeper into its bracken territory, and falling silent again.

Even in the dark, Brind knew where every dog was lying. He went through their names in his head, starting at the far end: Mace, Morningstar, Lance, Falchion. . . . Sir Edmund named all his hounds after weapons, except that sometimes he ran out of weapons and had to call them after other soldierly things instead. So there was a Hauberk, meaning "coat of mail," and a Bascinet, which was a kind of helmet.

But the leader of the pack was Glaive, which meant "broadsword." It was Glaive who had leaped at Brind in front of the cliff, and Glaive whose flank now provided his pillow.

Trebuchet, Haketon, Brown Bill, Spur, Dagger . . . Brind was drifting off to sleep again when he received a vicious twist of the ear. Tullo was leaning over him.

"Wake up, cur. You're going to war."

II

A HANDFUL OF GRAIN

The wagon jolted and Brind was thrown sideways among the dogs. He picked himself up and held on to the wooden bars at the side of the wagon, peering out at the slowly passing forest. The dogs pressed around him, buffeting each other for a spot where they, too, could stick out their heads and sniff the unfamiliar air. Glaive looked up at Brind. The dog's forehead was wrinkled, his brows raised, as if he were puzzled and seeking reassurance. They were a day away from home now, farther than the dogs, or Brind, had ever been. Tonight they would sleep at Arundel, which, according to Hatton, had a great castle. From there it would take two more days to reach Portsmouth. Unless it rained, in which case it would take three. Portsmouth, according to Hatton, was where the sea was. And the king.

Brind was beginning to feel sick from all the jolting and swaying. He didn't like traveling on wagons; he liked the ground under his toes. Liked to walk, lope, race unconfined. But Sir Edmund wanted to save the dogs' feet; not one of them was to be lame when they arrived in France. Not one. And if the dogs were to be cooped up, so was Brind, to keep them calm and steady. Tullo rode beside the wagon on his horse, cracking his whip at the bars to maintain his own kind of order.

Brind slumped on the wooden box that was chained to the wagon's floor and hung his head between his knees. He studied the grain of the lid to take his mind off feeling ill; ran his finger along to the heavy, new padlock. He didn't know what was in the box. It wasn't food, or he would be able to smell it and so would the dogs. Tullo had told him to mind his own business. Brind crawled urgently to the side of the wagon and was sick on the rutted, dry mud below. Glaive licked his face clean, and Brind hung on tightly to the comforting bulk of the dog.

He tried to think what Portsmouth might be like. And France, that strange country across the sea. But no pictures came into his head. And the sickness he felt in his stomach was in his heart as well. Sickness at being carried away from every- thing he knew: the sights and scents of home.

Brind clung more tightly still to Glaive and pressed his face against the dog's muzzle. What- ever happened on this uncomfortable, disturbing journey, at least they would be together. Dog and boy. Inseparable. And the dog didn't complain as Brind jerked forward and vomited again through the bars of the wagon.

Sir Edmund's horse sidestepped the sticky mess on the road. She was a fastidious, willful creature, but she would get him to Portsmouth. No good for the war itself, of course, but he had his chargers for that, his destriers. Three of them. Expensive great brutes that ate him out of house and home. He glanced around to make sure Philip was coping with them. Weedy, reedy Philip.

Sir Edmund had done his best to toughen up the boy since he'd been landed on him six years ago, but he should have been a monk, a scribe. Surprisingly good with horses, which was something, but he'd never make a warrior. And the surcoat he was wearing, with Sir Edmund's coat of arms on it, was far too big for him. It hung from his narrow shoulders like a flag on a pole, waiting limply for a breath of wind. Sir Edmund felt embarrassed. He didn't want to be a laughingstock when they rode in to the war muster at Portsmouth.

He considered the rest of his tiny band and found little comfort. Hatton trudged along at the head of the wagon team, with the willingness of a carthorse and the brain to match. Almost certainly he would be killed in the first battle. Tullo? He would fight like a maniac, Sir Edmund knew that. Tullo hated Frenchmen with a passion. Even though he'd never met one. And that left Brind, who was puking over the side of the wagon as if he were at sea already. If the Channel crossing proved difficult, he probably wouldn't survive it. That was the biggest worry. Sir Edmund needed Brind more than he needed any of the others.

"France?" asked Brind, pointing across the water at a low, dark line of land with humps behind it. The humps were turning pink in the last of the evening sun.

"No," chuckled Hatton. "That's the Isle of Wight." He had little knowledge but was proud of what he did have.

They were standing on the long shingle beach at Portsmouth, the sea in front of them, King Edward's war camp behind them. Brind didn't like the camp, so he kept his back to it as long as he could. There were too many sights, sounds, and smells, and all the time there were more. He had never seen so many men. So many faces. So many horses, wagons, tents, banners, cooking fires. The camp was like an ever-growing forest of color, smell, and noise. It was confusing, overwhelming. It agitated Brind, as it did the dogs. He could hear them barking now. They weren't the only dogs in the camp, but he could hear them clearly. Dagger, Brown Bill, and Glaive in full voice. Angry but in pain.

"Dogs, Hatton," said Brind anxiously.

He gathered up an armful of the driftwood they'd collected for their cooking fire and turned his back on the Isle of Wight. Hatton laughed and picked up the rest of the wood. He liked the war camp. He was going to like the war. His life had never been so exciting.

Brind ran through the camp, dodging around tents, ropes, and wagons, not looking for Sir Edmund's flag, just following the voices of the dogs. It was dusk now and firelight glowed on the faces of the soldiers crouched around their cooking pots. They laughed at Brind as he ran by and one stuck out a leg and sent him sprawling, then helped himself to the scattered driftwood as Brind got up and ran on without it.

A dozen of the mastiffs were tethered to the wheels of their wagon and were providing fine entertainment for the crowd who had gathered around. A tall knight and his huntsman were standing in front of the mastiffs with a pair of deer-hounds. Shaggy gray but long-legged and graceful, the deerhounds had no quarrel with the mastiffs but were being shoved toward them, provoking the tethered dogs so that they hurled them-selves forward repeatedly, their teeth flashing and snapping in anger and defiance, only to be choked hard as the leashes went taut and recoiled, flipping the mastiffs backward in heavy somersaults.

Sir Edmund and Philip were nowhere to be seen, but Tullo was there, close to the tall knight, baiting the mastiffs with the rest of the crowd, sharing the fun as Brind arrived. It was impossible for Brind's voice to be heard above the din. Instead, he felt inside his grubby tunic for a handful of the grain he always carried and threw it at Glaive, who was on his hind legs, neck bulging against the leash as he tried to reach his tormentors.

The shower of grain hit Glaive on his muzzle and the effect was instant. He dropped onto four feet and turned toward Brind, deerhounds and men immediately forbidden and forgotten. Brind barked once, a strange, throaty sound, and the other baited mastiffs, already distracted by Glaive's sudden change of mood, followed his example, groveling toward Brind, tails and bellies low. The dogs still in the wagon, who had been leaping and baying behind their bars, now wagged their tails and yelped hopefully, also trying to get close to Brind.

The watching crowd of men fell silent, then surprise gave way to an awed murmur and admiring laughter. All eyes were on the peculiar dog boy, who, without whip or stick or harsh words, had turned murderous hounds into lapdogs.

"Well, Tullo," said the tall knight quietly, though

the mockery in his voice was clear enough for all to hear. "Is this Sir Edmund's new master of hounds?"

The crowd's laughter filled Tullo's head and strangled his tongue. Only his hands could move, and he clenched his fists tighter and tighter.

"Bait them again, Tullo," said the tall knight. "If you can."

If you can. But Tullo dared not try. Dared not test his authority over the mastiffs, *his* mastiffs. Not here, not now, not in front of this sneering, arrogant beanpole with his fancy deerhounds and the bleating flock of sheep behind him. Not while the boy was there to distract the dogs. Always the boy. Always.

"They've been baited enough," Tullo heard himself say. "I was finished anyway."

"I should say you are." The tall knight smiled. "Next thing, you'll be boiled down for kennel meat."

And he sauntered off with his deerhounds, leaving the crowd to laugh at his wit, and at Tullo.

✦ ✦ ✦

When Sir Edmund returned from paying his respects to the Earl of Arundel, he could sense something was amiss, but Tullo said nothing about Brind's intervention. Yes, the dogs had been exercised, and yes, they had been baited. Sir Edmund approved of baiting. It kept dogs keen. Also, he was happy to think and talk dog after his interview with the earl, which had been uncomfortable, initially at least.

As expected, the earl had not been impressed with a war band of five, including two children and a carter. However, he had been impressed with the mastiffs, or the reputation that came before them. Sir Edmund had expressed the hope that his lordship would be even more impressed before the campaign was over, and the earl had smiled and clapped him on the back before sitting down to his dinner. True, he hadn't invited Sir Edmund to join him, but Sir Edmund didn't expect such favor. Not yet.

So he dined in solitary state in his own small, frayed tent, with Philip waiting on him and spilling the soup. And he listened to Tullo detailing the health and condition of every single mastiff from Bascinet to Trebuchet. And Tullo made no mention of the fact that he had baited the dogs far too cruelly. Or of his humiliation in front of the tall knight.

But in the small hours, when the camp was dark and silent, Tullo snatched Brind from his sleep beneath the wagon and beat him violently, without a word.

He had beaten the kennel boy many times before, but although Brind always accepted the treatment like a dog, he never truly seemed to fear Tullo, was never curlike, servile. It maddened Tullo. He could beat Brind, but not break him, and he perceived this as defiance. But Brind himself, curling up again beneath the wagon, bruised and bleeding, was neither defiant nor resentful. Tullo did what Tullo did. It was part of life in the kennels, like the frost that bit your nose in winter.

✦ ✦ ✦

Even Hatton was ready to leave the war camp by the time, two months later, it had become so big it spilled onto the ships that had gathered on the Solent. There were so many ships now, and so close together that they seemed to spread all the way across to the Isle of Wight like a bobbing wooden raft. Ships of all shapes and sizes — bought, borrowed, or simply taken by the king's men from merchants and fishermen in every port and harbor on the English coast.

It was a fleet, and an army, bigger than any that had ever before sailed from England. Fifteen thousand men, according to Hatton. He had no idea how many fifteen thousand actually was, but it certainly sounded like enough to conquer France. Though for another week Hatton conquered nothing, because the wind was wrong and the fleet remained at anchor. Hatton, and others of the fifteen thousand who were denied space on the open decks, simply heaved up and down in the stifling, cramped darkness below, listening to the ship's rats eating the army's corn.

+ + +

Before being brought to Portsmouth, Brind had never seen the sea. A man sometimes came to the manor selling fish called herrings that lived in the sea, but these were dry and chewy, not like the carp in the manor pond and the trout in its streams, which were tender and sweet. The man looked dry and chewy, too, and smelled like soup with too much salt in it that had gone bad. Brind had wondered if the sea would be like that: a bad, salty soup, stretching to the edge of the world. And when he'd first arrived at Portsmouth it had seemed so, except that it didn't stretch to the edge of the world because the Isle of Wight was in the way. But the sea had been calm then.

Later, when the wind shrieked through the camp and the waves piled up before crashing and seething on the shingle, it was different. Brind was terrified. The dogs were, too. At night the sea roared like a creature from hell. And now, with the wagon lashed to the deck of a wallowing bucket of a boat, turning out of the Solent into the gray, rolling nothingness, Brind and his hounds cowered behind their bars.

Sir Edmund stood alone on the deck — as alone as one could be in a crowded bucket. A little away from him a group of knights were amusing themselves by casting their hawks at the seagulls that glided hopefully above the fleet. Sir Edmund didn't care for hawking. Hawks were small, fiddly things that took ages to train and caught only birds or mice, which had never struck Sir Edmund as very exciting sport.

The tall knight was at the center of the group. Sir Edmund knew him vaguely: Sir Richard Baret. Relaxed, self-confident, a natural leader. Wealthier than Sir Edmund, younger, taller. Thinner. Sir Edmund straightened up and wiped the spray from his freshly painted shield, hoping the salt wouldn't damage it. The hounds were glossy black again and their field a lush green.

His real hounds, his mastiffs, weren't black at all. They were a brindled fawn color, except for their ears and muzzles and rings around their eyes. This discrepancy sometimes bothered Sir Edmund, who liked things to be right, but black stood out much more boldly on green than did brindled fawn. It was more dramatic. After all, it was more important to be recognizable on the battlefield than to use one's shield as an exact portrait of one's dogs.

Sir Edmund fretted about the dogs themselves. What if the crossing took a week, ten days? What kind of condition would they be in at the end of that? And was he right to leave the bitches at home? Would his neighbor Kempe be looking after them properly? Kempe. He wished the old man hadn't come to mind, because with him came Beatrice, who also, supposedly, was in his care while Sir Edmund was away.

Sir Edmund and his wife had parted coolly, but that was not Sir Edmund's fault. It *was* a just war. And even if it were not, it wasn't an *unjust* one. It was a war, plain and simple. Adventure, honor, perhaps plunder. Perhaps even a valuable captive for ransom. And God was on their side. God was definitely an Englishman. Even though the pope was French.

Beatrice hadn't argued back. Just looked unimpressed. And sad. But without war what would men of rank do, other than grow fat? Hunting was fun, it was exciting, exhilarating, but there was no honor in it, as there was in killing other men of rank. Killing, face-to-face, in a properly arranged battle, was the ultimate test of courage. Kill or be killed. It was simple, but the woman just couldn't or wouldn't understand.

Sir Edmund gripped the hilt of his sword, imagining that the white-crested waves careering toward the boat were French knights, all intent on killing him, an Englishman they didn't know. He didn't feel as excited as he thought he should. Perhaps he was just seasick again.

It wasn't Brind's fault. It was nobody's fault. The wagon was simply too heavy. The fleet had arrived at the Normandy coast of France and the army was wading ashore, while its baggage and supplies were ferried to the beach on lighters, flat-bottomed boats brought over for the purpose. It had been hard enough getting the mastiffs' wagon on board ship at Portsmouth. Now, lowering it more or less upright onto one of the lighters, with the sea swell causing everything to rise and fall, was almost impossible.

The dogs were still in the wagon and so was Brind. The mastiffs milled around excitedly, smelling land and eager to set foot on it, while Brind stood clutching the bars and staring down at the raised faces of Tullo and the other men on the lighter below—faces lifted closer and then taken away again as the swell dropped. The wagon swayed in space; boatmen shouted orders and advice at each other; and Hatton, still on deck with an anxious Sir Edmund, did his best to steady the load.

Then a rope snapped, Hatton yelled, and Brind's world turned upside down before going dark as the wagon dropped and tilted and forty mastiffs slid on top of him.

For an instant, Brind felt himself crushed and suffocated beneath the squealing, writhing mass. A ton of dog flesh pressed down on his face and chest until he thought he heard his ribs crack. But then the bars of the wagon gave way beneath his back, and Brind and the mastiffs avalanched into the sea below.

The broken wagon dangled over the side of the ship and Sir Edmund stared down in horror at the empty foam. Then the dogs began to reappear and Sir Edmund began to count them, hardly noticing Hatton leaping from the ship and hitting the sea like a slab of rock.

Deep in the opaque water, Brind twisted and kicked among the dogs, sharing their blind panic as they strove to surface. Hard-nailed feet scrabbled against his face and chest, unwittingly pushing him down, but at last he, too, burst into fresh air. Somewhere behind him he was aware of Hatton shouting at the dogs, herding them toward the shore. The dogs could swim. Brind could not. Then, floundering and sinking again, Brind felt teeth on his neck.

Thinking of the sea beasts that Hatton had told him about, he yelped and threshed his arms in terror. But the teeth became a wet muzzle against his cheek; Glaive was beside him. Brind grabbed at the dog, clung to his neck, and Glaive headed slowly but steadily for the beach. When Brind's knees finally hit land, he let go of Glaive and crawled the last few yards through the surf before collapsing on the wet, hard sand.

Glaive shook himself and stood over the boy, then growled and lowered his head. Tullo was already there, calling and whipping in the mastiffs as one by one they came out of the sea and galloped to and fro, reveling in being free of the cold, heavy water.

Hatton was wading ashore. He had lost one of his boots but didn't seem to notice.

"All safe, Tullo?" he gasped.

"All safe," said Tullo, dry as a bone. He looked at Hatton. "Didn't know you could swim."

Hatton laughed. "Never thought of that," he said, and shook his head. "I can't."

Tullo cracked his whip at the nearest dog and turned away.

It took two days and nights for every last soldier, every last barrel of beer, salted meat, and fish, and every last sack of grain and sheaf of arrows to be landed. Several horses broke their legs but Sir Edmund's all survived, and his mastiffs were unharmed. Miraculously. Further, the wagon had been rescued and an army carpenter had replaced the broken bars. The chains on the wagon floor had held firm, so the padlocked wooden box had not been lost to the deep.

Sir Edmund felt reassured. Content even. Certainly full. They had just dined on their first French wild boar. Hunted down by his mastiffs and expertly speared by his huntsman. Other knights had joined the hunt and had been very complimentary. Sir Edmund looked around at his people and felt guilty at having been ashamed of them on the road to Portsmouth.

When Hatton, sucking the last shreds of meat

from a boar's trotter, forgot his manners and asked unbidden across the fire, "Shall we kill a *two*-legged Frenchman tomorrow, my lord?" Sir Edmund simply smiled indulgently and nodded.

"A dozen of them, Hatton," he said. "And you shall have the boots off whichever one you choose."

Brind was in the wagon, grooming the mastiffs. He loved to comb their short hair till it glistened and felt smooth and supple to the touch. The dogs seemed to like it, too, and waited impatiently for their turn. As he worked, Brind's light from the cooking fire was suddenly blocked out, as if a cloud had passed over the moon, and looking up, he saw the silhouette of a man standing watching him. It was the tall knight. The silhouette nodded toward Brind with mock courtesy, then turned and walked on toward the fire.

A surprised Sir Edmund rose as the tall knight approached. Slightly flustered at being caught in the company of his servants, he signaled sharply for Hatton and Tullo to remove themselves from the fireside and murmured an order at Philip.

"Another chair."

"We haven't got one, sir," replied Philip.

"Then *find* one!"

Dismayed, Philip blundered urgently into the darkness. The tall knight bowed to Sir Edmund, who bowed back.

"Forgive me. I'm interrupting your dinner."

"No, no," replied Sir Edmund. "We—that is, I—had just finished."

There was no sign of the wretched Philip. Sir Edmund indicated his solitary chair.

"Please, do sit down."

With a swirl of his rich, heavy cloak, Sir Richard Baret sat down gracefully. The silver unicorns, freshly embroidered on his clean, new surcoat, pranced in the firelight.

Philip appeared, clutching a small barrel that smelled of fish, and looked helplessly at Sir Edmund, who glared at the barrel for an angry second, at Philip for two, then nodded curtly. Philip placed the barrel opposite Sir Richard.

"Some wine?" asked Sir Edmund politely, attempting to distract the tall knight's gaze and nostrils from the barrel.

"You are too kind, but no thank you." Sir Richard spoke easily, in the perfect aristocratic French of a courtier. It made Sir Edmund feel like a peasant.

"Leave us," Sir Edmund commanded Philip, wishing he could mean forever. Then he sat on the barrel, which wobbled, and smiled at Sir Richard, who smiled back.

What does he want? wondered Sir Edmund. Has he come just to amuse himself with the poor and lowly? Theoretically, Sir Edmund was of equal rank with the tall knight, but theory counted for little.

"A fine hunt today," said Sir Richard. "Good to get some exercise after being cooped up in that dreadful ship."

"Yes, indeed," replied Sir Edmund heartily, steadying himself on the barrel.

Sir Richard gazed into the fire.

"You will forgive me for saying so," he said at last, "but it has struck me that you are at a disadvantage on this campaign."

He looked at Sir Edmund and smiled. A tiny reflection of the fire twinkled in each of his dark eyes. Sir Edmund was confused.

"In what way exactly?" he asked.

"Your armor, sir. And your accoutrements."

Sir Richard glanced toward the tent. Outside it, Sir Edmund's chain mail, breastplate, and helm were propped up to dry after the sea crossing, together with his gauntlets and arm and leg guards, such as they were. His shield, big as a table, leaned against his lance, which was slightly warped. Sir Edmund followed the tall knight's gaze with mixed emotions. To a stranger this battle dress might well resemble a pile of scrap metal, but he liked to think it had served him well for many years. There was more to it than rust and worn-out buckles; there was history and tradition.

"There will be a great battle soon," said Sir Richard. "There has to be. The French king" —

he spat delicately into the fire — "must eventually come out and fight us. If he does not, he will have no country left to fight for. Or no country worth having."

Sir Edmund made to speak, but the tall knight seemed to guess what he was going to say and raised a hand as he continued smoothly.

"I do not for a moment doubt your courage, sir. I know you are ready to fight. None more so in this entire host. But a noble warrior should have equipment to match. In modern warfare it is essential. A full suit of plate armor, fluted armor, finely crafted, that will deflect arrows and sword points. And with such armor you would not need to carry that." He meant the great shield. "Two hands free, Sir Edmund. That means two Frenchmen killed instead of one."

He laughed, one warrior to another. Sir Edmund laughed, too, but he was completely lost now. A full suit of plate armor? Fluted? Finely crafted? Such stuff was made in Milan. It was obvious that Sir Edmund could never afford it.

Why was the man playing this game with him?

"So," smiled Sir Richard, "purely in the interests of killing more Frenchmen, and"—he nodded gravely, meaning Sir Edmund—"preserving the life of a noble friend, I should be honored if you would accept this."

He beckoned and, as Sir Edmund turned, Sir Richard's page appeared from nowhere. He was carrying, apparently without effort, a complete set of exquisite plate armor—enough to cover a man of Sir Edmund's size from head to toe without gaps, tucks, or protruding bits of leather and stuffed cloth. The helm's visor was elegantly pointed, unlike Sir Edmund's, which made him look like an ironclad pig. The whole effect was gorgeous and warlike in equal measure. Sir Edmund just stared.

"I am overwhelmed, sir," he said. And he was. Then he stood up, getting a grip on himself. "But I couldn't possibly . . ."

"Of course you could, man." Sir Richard laughed. "Why ever not? It's of no consequence to me. How many suits of armor can I wear? Take it, wear it, kill Frenchmen, be safe. It will warm my heart."

But Sir Edmund was shaking his head.

"It is too much, sir. As a gift. I should not feel honorable."

"But you do see reason?" pressed Sir Richard. "You see the advantage—no, the necessity—of such . . . fancy stuff?"

Sir Edmund nodded. "If it were mine, I should wear it, of course."

Sir Richard sat back with a sigh, smiling and shaking his head, as if both exasperated and impressed by Sir Edmund's quaint principles. He appeared to search a long while for a solution, then shrugged and leaned forward with another sigh.

"Very well, I see your objection. If you must give me something in return, so be it."

He shrugged again, then looked up at Sir Edmund as if the idea had only just come to him and really was the last thing he wanted.

"Give me the dog boy."

III

THE GREAT HUNT

Sir Edmund lay awake all night. The memory of the suit of fine armor shimmered above him in the roof of his tent. Once, when he dozed off for a moment, he dreamed that he was wearing it, and sat up with a start, feeling his arms and legs for smooth, fluted steel. When he fell back again on his prickly straw mattress, he was relieved that he was wearing only his undershirt. Because Brind was on his mind. On his conscience even. No, that was ridiculous. How could a kennel boy be on one's conscience? It would be like having a dog on one's conscience. A cow. A cat. A hayrick.

One didn't have a conscience about possessions. But Brind was certainly on his mind.

Sir Edmund had the finest pack of mastiffs in all of England. Would they be as fine without the boy? So eager? So responsive? Tullo had said often enough that the boy spoiled them. Perhaps he did. Perhaps they would be sharper, more obedient without Brind. Then why had Sir Edmund allowed Brind to grow up with the dogs? Why had he thought Brind vital to this adventure? Would it be insane to break the bond now or mere superstition to retain it?

After all, Beatrice surely would be overjoyed to know he had acquired better armor. The best. Not because she would be proud at the thought of him strutting about in it, but because he would be safer from harm. Did he not owe it to his concerned wife to accept the armor? The thought of owing a wife anything was as ridiculous as having a conscience about a kennel boy. But she would be pleased, he knew that.

Would she mind about Brind, though? In her

womanly way. Be concerned about his future? It was possible. But surely life for Brind with wealthy Sir Richard and his deerhounds would be far better than life at Dowe Manor. So exchanging Brind for the armor actually would be in the boy's interests. Wouldn't it? Even though it was nonsense to think in such terms.

Sir Edmund got up and strode out of his tent, wishing he could leave his overworked brain on his pillow. The grass was cold and clammy under his feet. Soon the camp would be awake and alive, but at this moment it seemed that Sir Edmund was the only waking soul. He walked silently toward the wagon. The dogs slept soundly, healthily tired out after the hunt. And Brind slept soundly too, beneath the wagon. Curled up against a wheel, just like a dog. A favorite dog.

Sir Richard took the rejection well—or, at least, politely. Sir Edmund didn't attempt to explain. He wasn't sure that he understood himself. He was a practical man who tried to have little time for instinct; but what else was it that made him keep a kennel boy and pass up a priceless suit of armor? Sir Richard's page laid the armor in a long polished box and closed the lid. Sir Edmund was reminded of a coffin and felt the back of his neck tingle cold at the thought.

The mastiffs' wagon lumbered south; one wagon in a baggage train of thousands, dragging along in the dust behind the army like a heavy tail, three miles long. Somewhere far ahead, the king and his knights and archers trampled and burned the countryside, so that Brind never saw fields, farms, and cottages. Every settlement was just a smell of burned thatch and burned crops by the time he and the mastiffs trundled past. France was not like England. It was blackened, smoking, and empty.

Hatton said they were marching across Normandy, and would march all the way to Paris unless the French king challenged them. In which case they would defeat him and then march on to Paris anyway. According to Hatton, the French ate horses and babies. He seemed particularly upset about the horses. This diet pleased the Devil, who therefore was on France's side. So, every time you killed a Frenchman, you killed a bit of the Devil. According to Hatton.

Brind didn't know what a battle was. He imagined it must be some kind of hunt. Sir Edmund considered trying to explain but decided against it. The boy wouldn't understand. Like the mastiffs, he responded to decent treatment and firm orders, not explanations. Brind thought like a dog. That was his strength, the reason he was here. There was no point in confusing him. Sir Edmund preferred simplicity: it was convenient. But it was also wrong. Brind understood dogs, which was not the same as thinking like one.

During the day, Brind saw little of Sir Edmund now, or of Tullo, who rode ahead with his lord and the other knights, as if he were a man-at-arms and not a servant. Sir Edmund didn't stop him: anything was better than the company of the puny

Philip. Tullo didn't seem to share Sir Edmund's disquiet at the daily destruction of the countryside. Good hunting ground was being laid waste, but if it meant that Frenchmen starved for want of game as well as crops and orchards, Tullo was quite happy. He'd become less concerned, too, at the lack of time and opportunity to exercise the dogs. Sir Edmund fretted at their being constantly confined except for a brief evening pull on the leash, but Tullo simply said they would be all the keener when they were finally let loose.

Two weeks after the English had landed in France, the city of Caen was attacked and taken, but Brind saw nothing except distant spires, which he knew were churches, and more smoke, which by now his nostrils had become used to. By the time the mastiffs' wagon arrived, the fighting was over.

Hatton felt cheated. He still had only one boot, and the makeshift replacement he'd made out of a grain sack was in tatters. Sir Edmund and Tullo had entered Caen too late to fight as well, because although they'd been far ahead of the baggage train, the bridge that had to be crossed to reach the city was narrow and there had been several thousand Englishmen ahead of them in the queue. Five hundred had been killed. Sir Edmund silently thanked God that he hadn't been one of them, and felt guilty for doing so. Brind wondered why a city in league with the Devil had so many churches.

For another two weeks after Caen the English army marched east toward Paris, then, quite suddenly, crossed a river and turned north. Brind knew he was traveling north: he felt the sun at his back now. He also sensed a difference in the baggage train. The difference was fear. Those on foot — the carpenters, the blacksmiths, the bowyers, the drovers, the women who had been collected along the way — walked more quickly now and talked less. From time to time Brind saw horsemen in the distance, keeping pace with the army. Watching like wolves.

Before long, Brind could smell the sea again. He

feared the sea but knew that home and his kennel were somewhere across it. Glaive stood panting beside him in the wagon. Brind stroked the dog's ears and hoped. But then, within sight of the beach, the army turned east again and the baggage train lurched, axle-deep, into another river. No bridge, just swift-running water and soldiers shouting at Hatton to hurry because the tide was rising. When the mastiffs' wagon ground its way up the chalky bank on the far side, Brind saw bodies lying along the river's edge. Dead horses and men with the water lapping against them.

That night there was relief and excitement in the English camp. Hatton said the French had tried to trap the English army but had failed. Now the French king would have to make a proper battle of it. There would be flags and trumpets and drums. He demonstrated to Brind how he would use his homemade weapon, a reaping hook lashed to a pole, to pull French knights from their horses. Armored knights would be wearing metal footwear rather than good leather boots, he supposed, but one couldn't have everything.

While Hatton lunged and hacked at imaginary Frenchmen, Sir Edmund stood with other knights in the Earl of Arundel's tent, listening to the latest information on the enemy. It seemed that, finally having stirred himself, the king of France was just twelve miles away and had gathered a war host five times larger than the English army. Sir Edmund glanced up to find Sir Richard Baret smiling at him.

"The armor can still be yours," said the tall knight quietly, implying that, at odds of five to one, Sir Edmund was going to need it.

But Sir Edmund shook his head. There could be no second thoughts. If the moment had come, that moment also belonged to Brind.

Two days later the English army streamed out of the forest and organized itself along a ridge above the village of Crécy. A valley sloped gently away in front of the ridge, wide, grassy, and free of trees. It was along this valley that the French army would come. The English sat down in the sultry August sunshine and waited. And waited.

For the first time since they had left the manor so many months ago, Hatton was separated from Brind and the mastiffs. He and his reaping hook were sent to join the ranks of the Welsh spearmen in the battle line. The Welshmen laughed at his sacking boot and at his hauberk, which was made of cracked leather rather than chain mail, but they gave him a rusty steel helmet, taken at Caen, to replace his leather cap, and shared their bread and cheese with him. And when the king rode along the line, Hatton rose to his feet and roared and cheered with the rest of them, like a proper soldier. At least, they said it was the king; he couldn't quite see.

Philip was fastening the buckles of Sir Edmund's armor and making a fumble-fingered job of it.

"For pity's sake, boy!" cried Sir Edmund, exasperated.

It wasn't Philip's fault. Sir Edmund had outgrown his breastplate and the buckle straps didn't quite meet across his back.

"You are too muscular, my lord," explained Philip. He meant fat but didn't say it.

"Pull harder!" shouted Sir Edmund.

Philip pulled harder and the strap broke. Sir Edmund controlled himself.

"Shall I fight naked, Philip? Would that be easier?"

Philip thought the sight of Sir Edmund naked would be certain to make the French run away but he didn't say that either. He improvised with a length of twine in place of the broken strap and pulled it so tight that Sir Edmund could barely breathe.

With the breastplate in place, plus arm, leg, and shoulder guards, Sir Edmund felt incredibly hot. He lowered his heavy pig helm over his head and felt himself suffocating. The visor refused to stay open. He pulled the helm off again and thrust it irritably at Philip. Just then the heavens opened and a heavy rain shower swept the ridge.

The rain caused momentary panic among the English archers, for wet bowstrings would be useless, but Sir Edmund raised his face to the downpour and felt refreshed. It was late afternoon now and he was tired. Perhaps the French army wouldn't come until tomorrow. But as the sudden rain ceased, so too did the chatter and shouting of the English soldiers. A hushed silence, as ominous as it was complete, spread along the entire battle line. Sir Edmund knew the French had arrived.

The English baggage and supply wagons were gathered behind the ridge, along with the army's horses, thousands of them, tethered and grazing, with no part to play; for the English were to fight on foot, their horses only to be used for pursuing the defeated French after the battle. Or to escape on, should the unimaginable happen and God deny King Edward victory.

Brind breathed in deeply the scent of the hillside grass after rain. Unlike all the others, the mastiffs' wagon still had its horse team in harness. The horses had stood patiently all day, heads swinging to and fro to escape the flies. But now, suddenly, Tullo was there, yanking at the lead horse so that it stumbled forward, and Brind, who had been confined to the wagon, was thrown to the floor by the sudden movement. Tullo was taking Brind and the dogs toward the ridge. Was this the great hunt at last?

Sir Edmund waited and watched the enemy. Philip stood close by with the pig helm and giant shield. The French army was winding into the valley below them: a colorful, even attractive, procession, with spear, axe, and armor glinting in the renewed sunshine. There were flags, trumpets, and drums, just as Hatton had gleefully predicted. All the deadly pageantry of war.

Sir Edmund was not a coward. He knew with absolute certainty that if his manor, his people, his wife, were attacked, he would defend them to the death. But on his previous campaign, eight years ago, he hadn't struck a single blow. The sea crossing from England had lasted ten dreadful days and, on landing in France, Sir Edmund had fallen seriously ill with a fever. At the time, he had feared it was the plague. It wasn't, but it left him too weak to stand. He was shipped back home, his insides and his honor just about intact. Sir Edmund had never killed a Frenchman. He had to put that right this time. Kill or be killed.

Still the French army poured into the valley: an endless river, rising toward the English. Like water uphill. Sir Edmund thought suddenly of Beatrice, but then he heard the mastiffs barking and the sound thrilled and encouraged him. Throwing his gauntlets at Philip, he pulled the small leather bag from his sword belt and strode away as fast as his armor would let him.

Tullo stopped the wagon just behind the battle line. He lashed at the bars with his whip to drive back the excited dogs before opening the door and climbing in, pushing Brind roughly from the padlocked wooden box. Then Sir Edmund was heaving himself into the wagon. He was clutching the leather bag and from it he took a small key, barely used. Sir Edmund was sweating and breathing hard, and his fingers shook as he guided the key into the padlock. The key turned and the padlock fell open. Sir Edmund threw back the lid of the box.

At first, Brind didn't understand what was inside or why it was there: iron spikes, piled like upturned teeth. Long, strong, and arrow-sharp. Then, as Sir Edmund and Tullo swiftly lifted them out, Brind saw that the spikes were on circles of iron. Collars. Collars for the dogs.

Behind them, a great roar rose from the English battle line. The French must have started their attack. Sir Edmund looked up at Brind and saw confusion and apprehension in his face. He should have tried to explain to the boy after all, but it was too late now. After the long day's wait, after the months of secret anticipation, everything was starting to happen too fast. He thrust a collar at Brind.

"Put them on the dogs, boy! Put them on!"

Brind and Tullo went from dog to dog, Tullo

bellowing and kicking at them so that they would be still, Brind growling softly at each one in turn. The mastiffs didn't like the collars but the iron was smooth, the fastenings well crafted, and soon every one of the forty had been turned into a dog of war. The wagon bristled with death.

"Leashes, leashes!" shouted Sir Edmund above the banging and chanting of the battle line.

Half a dozen men had arrived outside the wagon. They wore the livery of the Earl of Arundel. As Brind and Tullo put leashes to the iron collars and allowed the dogs, eager for freedom and edgy and aggressive from lack of it, to scramble toward the open door, the men backed fearfully away.

"They'll bite the French, not you!"

Tullo's voice was loud and contemptuous. He wouldn't mind if the mastiffs did take a lump out of the earl's men in their fancy black and gold checkers.

"Take Glaive!" cried Sir Edmund at Brind. "Lead the pack! Lead, lead!"

Sir Edmund's head was thumping. He could

hear the sharp snap of crossbow bolts hitting English shields. It was all running out of control; not like he had imagined and rehearsed it in his mind a thousand times. But still he was certain that Brind was the only one who could do this for him: keep the pack steady till the vital moment. Sir Edmund didn't want a yapping rabble; he wanted a disciplined force. Terrifying but disciplined. He wanted glory, for himself and for his dogs. The canine flower of chivalry. He knew the phrase was absurd, but their impact would not be. His mastiffs would bring down the fortune of France.

So Brind and Glaive marched into chaos. And Sir Edmund marched with them, great broadsword in hand, old-fashioned shield raised proudly, although it almost broke his collarbone. The ranks of archers and men-at-arms parted and roared encouragement and approval as the pack of mastiffs, his mastiffs, strained past, dragging the Earl of Arundel's leash men behind them. It was the finest moment of Sir Edmund's life.

Once at the front of the battle line, it was clear to Glaive and the rest of the dogs who was the enemy, the threatening intruder, the danger to survival. The entire English army was now the mastiffs' pack, to be protected; the ridge on which they stood was their territory, to be defended. The intruders in the valley must be driven off, destroyed. Glaive and his iron-spiked warriors snarled and bayed, rearing on their hind legs, desperate to kill.

"Hold, hold!" roared Sir Edmund at Brind and the earl's leash men.

The hail of crossbow bolts had petered out and now the French knights, on their great horses, were charging up the hill. Living, awe-inspiring war machines, trampling through their own crossbowmen as they came. Their formation was ragged at first, then they formed into tighter, menacing squadrons, heavy with armor and intent. Sir Edmund recognized some of the coats of arms on shield and surcoat: French lords of high rank, eager for honor or death. Let his dogs make it death.

"Hold, hold!" He raised his sword high. It seemed to weigh nothing. As did his shield.

Brind dug his heels into the rain-softened turf and clung to the leash. Despite the bond between them, the dog's natural wish to please the boy, Glaive was maddened to distraction by the approaching French. Their hooves shook the ground beneath his feet, their trumpets stabbed his eardrums, their men and horses smelled of blood. Brind suddenly lost his footing and Glaive was gone, dragging Brind, still clutching the leash, across the wet grass behind him.

Brind dug in his toes but they merely cut a narrow furrow of dirt as he slithered straight into the iron wave of French cavalry. Glaive leaped at the closest horse and Brind squealed as he felt his arms almost pulled from his shoulders. Then Glaive shrieked with a pain that Brind had never heard in him before and went on shrieking, and Brind lost his grip on the leash as dog and boy tumbled in flying mud beneath the hooves.

✦ ✦ ✦

Sir Edmund could only stare as Glaive and Brind were swallowed by the iron wave.

"Loose! Loose!" he cried, and the earl's leash men released the rest of the mastiffs. But their pack leader had gone and the dogs were confused in their fury, running madly in all directions. The French horses were too close now and wore too much armor. The dogs were slashed and kicked and slaughtered. They were an irrelevance. It had come to nothing. Sir Edmund had put his faith in Brind and Brind had failed him.

That was his last thought as the French knight with red falcons on his surcoat reared above him. Sir Edmund tried to raise his shield but it was too heavy. The falcons swooped and the Frenchman's sword smashed down.

Hatton neither saw nor heard what happened to the dogs. He was several hundred yards away. By the time the first rippling French charge reached the Welsh spearmen, he had shouldered his way into the front rank. He braced himself, as he had been taught, with the pole end of his homemade spear dug into the earth and the reaping-hook end angled toward the enemy. This meant that the French horses would be stopped in their tracks. Then you could hack and lunge and help yourself to boots. Hatton had his eyes fixed on a knight on a black horse. The knight was dressed finely in blue and gold, though Hatton couldn't see his footwear. He was surprised and disappointed when another horseman crunched straight through his home-made spear. And straight through his cracked leather hauberk.

Brind followed the trail of blood. He knew it was Glaive's blood. He couldn't see Glaive but his scent was still strong. The disorientated dog was some-where across the slope, crawling toward the sanc-tuary of the forest. Brind ran after him. One of his arms didn't work and his toenails were torn, but it wasn't the pain that made him whimper as he ran.

He fell to the ground and sheltered behind a dead horse as the next squadrons of French cavalry galloped over him, churning the ground and shouting death at the English army above. Brind ran on.

From the battle line, Tullo, free of dogs and master, watched him go, and spat; then swung his axe at a Frenchman he'd never met. How he hated Frenchmen.

In the forest, Brind could still hear the noise of the great hunt. The cries of the horses chilled his blood and the drums made an everlasting thunder that never broke into rain. The trees were still dripping from the earlier shower and the smells of the forest were heady because of it, but they gave Brind no comfort. He remembered running with Glaive through the forests of home. The pursuits ending in licking and laughter. Now he was the pursuer and Glaive the quarry. But he could see no sign and had lost the scent.

The sun was dipping behind the ridge and suddenly the unfamiliar forest became stranger still as shadows filled hollows and changed shapes.

Brind didn't fear the dark, but he feared separation from Glaive. He cast around, then headed deeper into the forest.

By midnight Brind was exhausted and almost without hope. Twice he had caught the faintest scent, and once had thought he'd heard Glaive's voice, far off, but it had led him nowhere. Now he decided that he should go back to the English camp. The other dogs needed him. He could hear no sound of the great hunt now, either because it was over or because he was too far away.

When Brind finally emerged from the forest, the valley and ridge were moonlit and quiet. The slope was littered with dark lumps, like outcrops of rock, but Brind had seen enough of the great hunt to realize the lumps were not rocks but the bodies of horses and men. As he made his way uphill, the bodies were piled higher. Scattered among the piles were the remains of the other mastiffs. Brind found all thirty-nine dogs, although he couldn't recognize them all. He couldn't recognize Hatton at first either. Then he saw the sacking on his foot.

There were plenty of English soldiers around but they took no notice of Brind. They were relaxed, laughing, celebrating victory. But there was no sign of Sir Edmund. Brind knew Hatton was dead. Was Sir Edmund dead, too? He found the empty wagon, the lid of the wooden box still open. The horse team stood sleeping. Brind stroked the lead horse as if it might speak to him, then yelped in agony as a hand gripped his damaged shoulder. Brind knew the hand. It squeezed harder, realizing the pain it was causing.

"What have you come back for?" breathed Tullo in Brind's ear. "Eh? Coward. Treacherous little cur. D'you know what happens to traitors?"

He moved his free hand and Brind heard the steel before he saw it, then felt it cold against his neck.

Brind jerked his head and sank his teeth into Tullo's wrist until he could feel bone and taste blood. And he didn't let go, even after Tullo had dropped the knife. Suddenly he wanted to hurt Tullo, to repay him for all the hurting Tullo had ever done to him, and to the mastiffs. He wanted to hang there, biting forever.

But the thought was new and confusing and didn't make him happy, for Brind had never wanted to hurt anyone before, and when Glaive came back into his mind, he ran. Back across the bloodied slope. Back through the forest. He ran until he could run no further and then he sprawled face down in the wet leaf mold of the forest floor, panting and sobbing.

Eventually, Brind got to his knees and howled at the night. But there was no answer.

IV

AURÉLIE

The girl was only ten years old. Her father was dead, her mother was ill, and her grandfather was feeble, so when the soldiers hammered at the door the girl knew what to expect. She was not a fool. Her mother and grandfather went without protest. The old man didn't know what was happening and her mother was too sick to care. But the girl scratched the face of the soldier who grabbed her arm, kicked another, and spat in the face of a third. The soldiers just laughed and pulled her out of the house. One suggested they give her a sword and put her on the town wall with the rest of the garrison, but their captain shook his head. He believed only men and boys could fight. Girls were a nuisance. So she was herded to the town gates with the others.

Five thousand people lived in the town of Calais and two thousand of them were now penned by the gates: the young, the sick, the old, the female. Because the town was besieged — surrounded — every scrap of food was needed for those considered fit and strong enough to defend it. The rest were just a burden: two thousand useless mouths.

The heavy gates creaked open and the useless mouths were prodded and pushed outside to meet their fate. Some wept and pleaded, but for the most part they went silently: a few erect and proud despite their rejection, the rest simply shocked or uncomprehending. The girl was fierce inside but held her mother's hand. The hand was cold and thin. The girl's father had gone to fight the English but now the English were here. He had died for nothing, and her mother seemed to be dying, too.

The town gates closed behind them and the girl heard the great wooden bar fall into place. The other useless mouths also heard it and stood as one for a moment, lost and unwanted, between the walls of the town that was no longer their home and the line of flags and tents that was their enemy. Then those who could walk straggled cautiously toward the English, because they'd been told that King Edward would be chivalrous and give them bread and safe passage through his lines.

Safe passage to what? thought the girl. Starvation in our own countryside? The English had already stripped it clean. They were locusts. Pigs. Locust pigs. Anger tightened her grip on her mother's hand. But her mother seemed grateful enough for the bread. In truth, it was as good as they'd had inside the town for some time. And her grandfather was happy with it, too. He was always happy when he was eating. Otherwise, he wandered around mumbling earnestly to himself, as if looking for something important that he'd lost. He could never explain what it was, so the girl had given up asking. Perhaps he was looking for his wits, but that was a cruel thought and the girl knew it. But she didn't love her grandfather. He would probably die when the winter came and the girl couldn't pretend she would be sorry.

She wasn't sure she loved her mother either. Her mother was gentle but she was weak. Even before she'd become ill, even while her husband was alive, she had infuriated the girl by her acceptance of everything. They had both loved the husband-father, but whereas after his death the girl's deep grief had turned into strength, her mother was wasting away. The girl wanted revenge; her mother had settled for the enemy's moldy bread.

And now her mother had wandered back vaguely toward the town walls and was sitting down, as if to wait. For what? The gates to open and readmit her? The English to march away, tossing herrings and beans to her as they went? She was not alone either. The girl was ashamed to see so many useless mouths lingering like her mother, with or without hope, certainly without purpose. The girl wanted to shout at them, rally them, form an army of them. Instead, she waited until dark, then slipped away.

She was able to leave a note for her mother because she'd had a little education and could write. The note was scratched in charcoal on the girl's linen cap:

MOTHER
I AM A BURDEN TO YOU
I HAVE GONE
AURÉLIE

The locust-pig sentries were easy to evade, but once past them Aurélie had to think. If she were not to be as aimless as the other useless mouths, she needed a direction in which to march. North would lead her straight into the sea, and she wasn't yet ready to invade England single-handed. So she decided to turn south. That way she should meet up with bits of the defeated French army, which had been badly let down at Crécy, so it was said, by its crossbowmen, who weren't French at all but came from Genoa. The army would regroup, then march on Calais and sweep the English into the sea. Aurélie would be part of that army.

Brind had been searching the forest for many days and nights now. His shoulder grew less painful, although stiff, and he didn't starve because it was autumn and there were plenty of berries and also mushrooms. One kind of mushroom made him very sick, so sick that all he could do was curl up in the roots of a tree and wait until he felt better or died. He didn't die, but he didn't eat that kind of mushroom again.

And all the time his only thought was to find Glaive. He didn't know how far he had traveled from Crécy in his search, for the forest was thick and there were no landmarks other than the occasional fallen tree. The sun, when he could see it through the clouds or the leaf canopy, gave him clues to his direction; but when he couldn't see it, he might well have been going around in circles. It was so different from the forests of home, where Brind knew every twig, every root, and where, when he called or barked, a dog called back. Here, the forest continued to ignore him.

During the day, there was only birdsong or silence; and at night, the careful, secret noises of wild animals going about their business. Badgers and hedgehogs would snuffle at him briefly, then patter on their way. Once he woke suddenly, convinced he could hear Glaive approaching, but it was only a fox, which stared at him a moment and then left, like the badgers and hedgehogs, careless of Brind's desolation.

The dog boy was entirely alone. When he wasn't thinking about Glaive, the memory of the great hunt filled his mind. That and Tullo. The sudden, brief desire he had felt to hurt the huntsman still disturbed him. He desperately wanted the comfort, the reassurance of Glaive at his side.

Then, late one evening, Brind heard a new noise. He stood quite still, listening, locating. Raised his head and scented the dusky air. A human scent. A human noise. Somebody crying. Brind crept through the undergrowth, following his ears and nose.

✦ ✦ ✦

Aurélie had collapsed. She wasn't ready to rest, but the sense of purpose that had propelled her away from Calais, away from her mother, had deserted her, to be replaced by mere frustration and guilt. Frustration that she couldn't find the French army, and guilt that she'd abandoned her mother. In her note she'd said that it was she, Aurélie, who was the burden, but that was a lie. Aurélie had felt her mother was a burden and had wanted to be free. Free to fight. To avenge her father. How vain, how foolish, how selfish! But there was no way back now. She bit hard into a piece of wood on the mossy bank where she'd thrown herself and hoped it would break her teeth as punishment; but the wood was rotten and fell apart in her mouth, making her choke.

Aurélie sat up, spitting out wet bark and woodlice, her eyes streaming. And then she saw the boy looking at her. At least, she thought he was a boy. The way he was crouching, on his haunches, made him look more like an animal, ready to spring. And his tunic and breeches were brown and shabby, like the hide of a mangy wild dog. A dog. Yes. His dirty face was dark and slightly upturned; his teeth looked sharp. Despite herself, Aurélie shrank away. But the dog boy seemed as wary as she was. Finally, he spoke. Or barked.

"Dog?"

Aurélie didn't understand.

"Dog?" he asked again.

She understood this time. It was definitely a word, not just a sound. In Norman French, with a very rough accent. Was he asking if she was a dog? Was he mad? Aurélie shrank away a little further.

"Have you seen dog?" asked the boy.

Aurélie shook her head.

"Big. Fine. Mastiff. Glaive." He repeated the last word and lowered his dark eyes.

"No," said Aurélie, in her clear Norman French, far better than the boy's. "I haven't seen a dog."

"Glaive hurt," the boy growled softly. He looked sad.

"Your dog?" asked Aurélie.

The boy nodded, then shook his head, correcting himself.

"Master's."

Aurélie straightened up.

"Who is your master?" she asked quickly. "Does he live near here?"

The boy shook his head again. "England."

England? *England!* Aurélie felt the anger rush back into her.

"You come from England?" she asked.

The boy nodded. "With Glaive. With dogs. With Sir Edmund."

Aurélie sprang at him with teeth and nails bared. A wild cat tearing at a wild dog. A stinking English wild dog! The boy yelped and tried to push her off, fending her snarling face from his neck, grabbing at her wrists to keep the long nails from slashing him. She managed to draw blood, but the boy was stronger than she was and wriggled and twisted and pushed her over so he was kneeling on her legs and had both her wrists gripped tight. Aurélie burst into tears and the boy leaped back from her in alarm. He watched from a safe distance, cautious but apparently concerned, as she sat there, streaked with mud and moss, and sobbed her heart out.

When, finally, the sobbing had dried up into great hiccuping breaths, the boy edged slowly forward. He stroked Aurélie's hands and head as if she too were a dog. His lost dog, Grave, or whatever its name was. Aurélie didn't object. Comfort had been lacking in her life a long time.

Close up, the boy smelled like a dog; and he was English. But she had tried to kill him and now he was gently stroking her hair. Aurélie hadn't slept properly since running away. She slept now, utterly exhausted, curled up in the mossy hollow, with the dog boy close by, while the badgers and hedgehogs snuffled past unnoticed.

When Aurélie woke at dawn, the boy had gone. But before she could decide whether she was glad or sorry, he was back with a handful of blackberries and a honeycomb. He seemed particularly proud of the honeycomb, and pointed, grinning, at the red bumps on his arms where the bees had stung him as he'd raided their tree. Aurélie ate nearly all the honeycomb and felt guilty afterward, but it was her first food since leaving Calais; she was literally starving.

Now Aurélie had to make a decision. The boy was looking for a dog; she was looking for an army. It was unlikely the two would be in the same place. So, must she continue on her own? She didn't like the forest. She would be much better off with the dog boy, who could find bees' nests and didn't mind getting stung. But what if they met the French army before they found the dog? If that happened, Aurélie decided, she would plead for mercy on the boy's behalf; ask them not to kill him. It would be a very gracious thing to do. She licked honey from her fingers and looked forward to it.

"What's your name?" she asked.

"Brind."

"Mine's Aurélie."

The boy didn't seem interested. "Find Glaive," he said.

He stood up, ready to move. Obviously he expected her to come too.

"I'm ready," said Aurélie, cramming the last of the blackberries into her mouth. But she didn't mention the French army.

Soon after they'd set off, it started to rain: large gentle drops, plopping through the leaves. Aurélie stuck out her tongue to catch them. Before it became heavy, the rain enlarged all the smells of the forest again and Brind stopped every few paces to sniff around him. But the one scent he longed to pick up wasn't there. When the rain came on harder and settled in, Aurélie became sullen and then cross. The dog boy seemed waterproof: the rain formed beads on his hair and tunic without soaking either, and his bare feet squelched easily through the mud. Aurélie's sodden dress clung to her heavily and chafed her shoulders; and water ran off her flattened hair into her eyes in the most irritating way.

When they came across a tumbledown hut, once built of turf and thatch, she insisted they take shelter, and they sat huddled in silence on the one dry patch of floor. Brind was thinking of the warm, sweet bracken in the sleeping lodge at home; Aurélie wondering if it was raining at Calais and, if so, whether her mother had found shelter.

Aurélie heard the hooves before Brind did, perhaps because he was listening only for a dog. She suddenly gripped his arm. Brind listened and he too heard the noise; some way off but getting closer. Hooves and harness. And the hooves were striking stone, not soft forest floor.

"A road," hissed Aurélie. "We're near a road. It's the army!"

She scrambled to her feet and ducked out of the shelter, rattailed hair and waterlogged dress forgotten. Brind followed. He hadn't grasped what Aurélie had said about the army but he was willing to find a road and speak to horsemen. They might have news of Glaive.

The rain had almost stopped but the undergrowth slapped at Aurélie like wet seaweed as she ran toward the growing noise of hooves. So many of them! It *must* be the army. Brind was close behind her as they tumbled out onto the road in front of the leading horse, a fine gray destrier, which reared and skittered sideways in surprise. Its rider, a tall knight in fine armor and equally fine cloak, curbed the horse expertly.

Aurélie frowned up at the knight. She knew by heart the coats of arms of almost every nobleman in France, but she had never seen silver unicorns on a field of blue. The knight wasn't returning her stare. He was looking straight past her, at the dog boy. Brind found himself face-to-face with Sir Richard Baret.

The tall knight must have been astonished to meet Brind on this wet, lonely road but he didn't show it. Still patting and quieting his horse, he bowed with his familiar mock courtesy.

"Well, well, Brind." He smiled. "What a lucky young coward you are."

Aurélie turned sharply on Brind. "Coward?"

It was the biggest insult she could imagine, the most despicable thing to be.

"He ran from the battlefield," Sir Richard explained politely, as if Aurélie were a highborn lady, rather than a bedraggled ten-year-old.

"But now he is rescued. Unlike poor Sir Edmund."

He shook his head sadly, then shrugged.

"But there, one man's misfortune is another's . . . opportunity."

Before Brind or Aurélie could react, Sir Richard jabbed the short lance he was carrying at Brind and speared the thick collar of his tunic. He lifted Brind from the ground and held him in mid-air, twitching like a hooked fish, while two of his men-at-arms swiftly dismounted. And then Brind felt strong hands grabbing him as Sir Richard jerked the lance free.

"You should have cost me a second-best suit

of armor," said Sir Richard. "Now you cost me nothing. War does have its compensations. Bring the girl as well."

Aurélie had soon realized she had blundered into an English war band and not the French army. But the fact that the tall knight seemed to know Brind, and that Brind was somehow valuable, had kept her rooted. Not to mention the sudden hoisting of Brind on the lance. Now it was too late to run. She spat and kicked and pummeled instead, but the English soldiers were just like the French ones in Calais. They simply laughed at her and carried her away.

Brind was utterly bewildered. He'd had no knowledge at all of Sir Richard's interest in owning him, or of a suit of armor being offered. The idea was beyond him. And now he and Aurélie had been slung over a pack horse and tied down like deer carcasses. They were prisoners. Why? Then he heard the deerhounds.

Sir Richard Baret was a gentleman. When finally Brind and Aurélie were lifted from the pack horse and untied, he apologized to Aurélie, though not to Brind, for the uncomfortable ride. Speed had been essential, miles needed to be covered, contact with the enemy maintained. He apologized to Aurélie for the fact that the French *were* the enemy. It was merely an accident of birth and he personally knew and admired many Frenchmen. He also apologized when he set her to light the fire and cook dinner. Two of his cooks had died on the campaign; it was a habit cooks had and was most inconvenient. But there were only fifty men to feed. He was sure she would manage.

Aurélie said nothing and didn't try to escape. She would eat some bread, put dung in the stew, kill Sir Richard, and then run away.

While Aurélie plucked French chickens stolen by the locust-pig English, Brind was meeting the deerhounds. If Sir Edmund Dowe had been fond and proud of his mastiffs, he had never lost sight of the fact that they were dogs. Sir Richard Baret treated his deerhounds as if they were princes.

There were just ten of them and they traveled in luxury. The floor of their wagon was strewn daily with fresh bracken or straw; their bodies shaded by velvet curtains which could be unfurled against the sun; their thirst quenched at will from polished pewter basins mounted at each end of the wagon. Their huntsman was more in the nature of a personal valet, ministering to their needs. And the tall, elegant hounds were as polite as their master: as Sir Richard introduced them individually to Brind by name, each lowered itself silently to the floor of the wagon. They made Brind's mastiffs seem like bulky bruisers, ruffians. But although they were pampered, how the deerhounds could run.

Sir Richard took Brind, the hounds, and his hunts-man to an open hillside behind the camp. He said it was perfectly safe: this part of France had been cleared of French. The hounds wore finely worked leather collars that matched their gray-blue hair, and their leashes were smooth to the touch, not like the broad, rough straps that Brind's mastiffs used to strain at.

The huntsman was sent hurrying off across the slope, which reminded Brind of the valley at Crécy. It made him think of the dead mastiffs, and it made him think of Glaive. His eyes prickled and he panted for breath. Sir Richard was speaking but he didn't hear. Then Sir Richard kicked him.

"Loose them, boy. Let them go!"

Sir Richard had unleashed the deerhounds he was holding. Brind unleashed the rest and they lunged away after the others; like a trace of gray smoke, streaking across the hillside. In the distance, against the forest edge, Brind could see the huntsman. The line of gray smoke curved toward him. The deerhounds seemed to float just above the grass rather than run across it.

"Are they beautiful, Brind?" asked Sir Richard, watching the dogs raptly. "Are they beautiful?" he repeated.

Brind could see only Glaive, dragging himself from the mangled nightmare of the great hunt. Sir

Richard cuffed him, not viciously, as Tullo would have done, but with a certain impatience.

"Are they beautiful?" he repeated.

Brind nodded.

"Yes, my lord," suggested Sir Richard, and he looked at Brind.

"Yes, my lord," growled Brind.

Sir Richard nodded approvingly.

"I am your lord now," he said. "You are part of my pack. And when we return to England, you will live in my kennels. Do you still have the magic grain?"

He smiled at Brind, who didn't immediately understand.

"The grain, boy. Portsmouth? The war camp? You threw grain to control the mastiffs. They ignored Tullo and came to you on their bellies. Grain!"

Brind obediently felt inside his tunic and held out a handful of corn. He had replaced it after falling in the sea, but this new supply was also mildewed, from his many nights in the forest. Sir

Richard looked at the rotten handful with mock distaste.

"There will be dry corn in England," he said. "And a new litter of hounds on which to work your magic."

There was no magic involved as far as Brind was concerned. He had learned early in life that by distracting a dog you stopped it doing what it was doing. You didn't need to kick or beat it. The sudden tingle of corn on its muzzle meant "Stop." It was simple, as was Brind's place as natural leader; but Brind didn't have the words to explain. He just shook his head.

"No magic," he said.

"Well, we won't tell the king that," said Sir Richard, smiling, "when he comes to visit. We'll put on a fine hunt for him. The hounds will have a stag at bay, then you'll throw your magic corn and they'll trot off home behind you without a backward glance. The king will make me a duke on the spot. The Duke of Deerhound."

He laughed, then looked at Brind.

"You'll have to have some decent clothes, of course. A uniform."

He tapped a finger at the silver unicorns on his surcoat. In the distance, the deerhounds had reached the huntsman and were milling around him. He looked like a tiny rock in a small gray sea.

"Call them," said Sir Richard, without looking at Brind. Another cuff. "Call them."

Brind gazed toward the hounds. He saw Glaive again, damaged and limping. He threw back his head and howled.

The stew was good. Everybody agreed. And the roast chicken too. But then, the French were supposed to have a certain flair for such things, so it was no less than they expected. Still, the men-at-arms who dined with Sir Richard all congratulated him on acquiring such an excellent cook. Sir Richard gave Aurélie a gracious nod of mock gratitude. Aurélie wished she could skewer him with the roasting spit.

She had failed to spoil the stew with dung

because two soldiers had been posted to watch her every move. She had failed even to burn the chickens because one of the soldiers turned the spit every time she pretended to forget it. The dinner was good and she was a failure. The thought of having prepared a delicious feast for the English locust pigs while her mother starved outside the walls of Calais was almost too much to bear.

Brind and the deerhounds were fed the scraps. Aurélie hoped the dog boy would choke on a bone. His future suddenly seemed secure to Aurélie: snuggled up with his fancy new dogs; his old one, Grave, or whatever its name was, forgotten. He was indeed a lucky coward. And Aurélie was a slave. A stupid, stupid slave. She was on her own again.

That night, Aurélie was tethered to a tree, but she'd expected that and was prepared. The small, sharp knife she'd stolen from the camp kitchen was hidden inside her stocking. It pricked her ankle reassuringly. It was just a question of when to go, what damage to do first, and what to take. She had to take something besides the knife. The knife was probably English; she wanted something French. Something the locust pigs had stolen during their fighting and destroying.

And she would kill Sir Richard. Should she kill the rest, though? Perhaps not. Being English, they would die noisily and she would be caught. Just Sir Richard, then. But Sir Richard's tent was near the horses. Aurélie didn't like horses and they didn't like her. They would make a noise too. She wished she'd used the roasting spit when Sir Richard had been sitting smirking by the fire. It would have been so much easier. And she was getting too tired to think.

When Aurélie woke, she was damp with dew. She had dreamed that she'd escaped and was floating across the forest toward the French king. But she hadn't escaped; she was still tethered to the tree. The knife had cut her ankle and her stocking was sticky with blood. Worse, much worse, the sun was about to rise. Broad daylight was minutes away.

Aurélie made herself sit still for a few seconds. She had to be quick but she had to be quiet; very quiet. She tugged the knife from her stocking and sawed at the double knot which bound the rope to her other wrist. It would have been quicker to leave the knot and just cut the rope somewhere between her wrist and the tree, but Aurélie wasn't leaving with any sign of English slavery still on her.

When the knotted rope finally fell to the ground, Aurélie rubbed her wrist and stood up. She knew that most of what the English had stolen, their plunder, would be stowed in the baggage wagon; but three soldiers sleeping near the fire had their packs with them. Perhaps just for use as pillows; perhaps because they had reason for keeping them close.

Aurélie crept toward the men. Two of them were snoring and, although disgusted, she was glad of the noise they made as she crouched by the nearest and sliced through the binding that secured his pack. It turned out to contain nothing more than a tightly rolled bundle of dank, dirty clothing. The man's neighbor looked more promising: the pack was larger, more solid. Aurélie cut, unrolled, and rummaged. A few coins chinked loudly; a small golden cup rolled out. But it wasn't these that caused Aurélie's heart to stop.

For several seconds she was unable to breathe. Then she picked up the brooch. It was sea green in a setting of silver wire. Not a woman's brooch. It was large and heavy. For fastening a heavy cloak. A man's brooch. Her father's.

V

BETONY

Aurélie's scream would have woken the dead; it certainly woke the English. The soldiers snoring by the fire scrambled to their feet and Sir Richard strode frowning from his tent. Throughout the camp, bleary soldiers grabbed their swords and ran toward the sound.

Aurélie screamed again. She heard herself this time but was incapable of movement. She still clutched the brooch. The soldier from whose pack she'd taken it was standing facing her. He wasn't a monster; just a young man who'd gone to war to seek his fortune, and found a piece of jewelery on a dead man's body. He couldn't have known that Aurélie was that man's daughter, but such was the force of her shock and outrage that suddenly he felt ashamed and couldn't strike her down.

His two companions had no such scruples. They pushed him aside, one grabbing at Aurélie, the other swinging at her legs with a heavy club. Aurélie sprang sideways, pushed a cooking pot in their way, and fled.

Brind was already awake when he heard the first scream. Aurélie confused him—pleasant one moment, angry and unkind the next—but the scream was not one of bad temper.

Unlike Aurélie, Brind hadn't been tethered: Sir Richard was sure of him. Sir Richard was mistaken. The deerhounds watched from their wagon with dignified interest as Brind ran off.

Whatever her plans had been the night before, Aurélie wasn't intending to cause havoc now: she was just trying to escape. But she had turned the wrong way and was stumbling around the camp rather than sprinting away from it. It was hard to sprint through a tent. Her pursuers became as entangled as she did, though, and the kitchen knife was still sharp, so she was able to cut through rope and canvas when there seemed no way forward.

Brind was trying to reach Aurélie. It was clear she was being hunted and there could be only one outcome if she were caught. When he lost sight of her he tried to catch her scent, but it was impossible in the stirred-up air. He turned away and ran toward the horses instead.

Sir Richard had relaxed. On discovering the commotion was not an attack by the French but an escape bid by the girl, he had laughed indulgently and let things take their course. He would have to intervene if he didn't want her killed, but his lumbering troops had to catch her first. The sudden noise of horses surprised him and he spun around, fearful that the French were attacking after all. But the horses galloping into the confusion were riderless. They were his own and his men's. Somebody had untethered them and was driving them through the camp. Sir Richard glimpsed a dark head and a brown tunic lit up by the rising sun.

Aurélie was as scared of the panicked horses plunging around her as she was of the English soldiers, who now were trying to contain them without getting kicked. When a hand grabbed her wrist, she squealed. Brind simply dragged her away toward the forest.

In the trees they paused for breath. Aurélie was trembling and still clutching the kitchen knife in one hand, the brooch in the other. Brind thought she was about to start sobbing again but she didn't, and when he tried to take the brooch, so she would have a hand free, she held it tighter and glared at him fiercely. Brind pointed inside his tunic.

"Safe," he said.

Already he could hear the horsemen coming. There was no time to argue. He tore the brooch from Aurélie, stuffed it inside his tunic, and gripped her hand tight.

"Run!" he barked.

Aurélie ran, or rather allowed herself to be dragged like a rag doll. She too could hear the horses behind them now. And the shouts of their English riders. Angry, threatening shouts.

The forest itself seemed to Aurélie to be her enemy, too, rather than her friend; all gloom and obstacles. She hated forests. She wished she weren't earthbound, with bursting lungs. She wished she could fly over the forest, as in her dream. So when, without warning, her feet left the ground, she was agreeably surprised. But she was falling rather than flying.

Sir Richard's horse sensed the edge of the ravine before Sir Richard did, and the tall knight was grateful for it. The horse balked and shied away, almost unseating its rider, and the rest of the horsemen came to a similar, shuddering halt.

The ravine was little more than a cleft, with bushes and brambles clinging to and concealing its edge. From somewhere below, the English soldiers could hear running water. Apart from that, and the snorting of the horses, there was silence.

Sir Richard signaled for his men to spread out and they cautiously sidestepped their horses along the top of the ravine, peering down through the leaves of the feeble trees that reached up from the perpetual shade below. Sir Richard himself dismounted and clambered a little way down. It was impossible for a human being to climb farther, down or up.

He was wondering whether to summon his deerhounds when he glimpsed something lying in the narrow stream below, half hidden by rocks. He edged farther along for a better view and felt a pang of real disappointment when he recognized the brown tunic and dark head. Both the tunic and the head, which was face down in the water, were motionless, and remained so. Blood clouded the stream.

Sir Richard stood gazing down for several minutes. There was no sign of the girl. Probably she was dead too; she wouldn't be able to keep quiet if she were merely injured. It didn't matter about the girl anyway. Only the dog boy. Sir Richard allowed himself to hurl a stone down into the stream to relieve his feelings, then hauled himself back onto his horse.

Brind lay completely still for a very long time. Long after the sound of horsemen had ceased. The stream gurgled around him, as if he were just another rock. His forehead was in the water, but his nose and mouth were in a hollow of mud and stones in which, face down, he could still breathe, just, though he could taste the mud. He had scooped the hollow when he'd heard the horsemen arriving up above, levering out a small rock from the streambed with his fingers. The hollow had started filling again almost immediately. Now it was full, water touching his nose and lips. He had to move or drown.

Brind turned his head slightly sideways, trying not to splutter. There was no reaction from above. He waited a few more seconds, then struggled to his feet. Water poured from his tunic and blood trickled from a gash above his eyebrow, but nobody shouted from the top of the ravine. Sir Richard and his men had gone.

Brind remembered Aurélie. Although he'd struck his head when finally bouncing into the stream, he otherwise felt remarkably unhurt; the trees had broken his fall. Had Aurélie been as fortunate? He looked along the narrow ravine but couldn't see her. Although the horsemen had gone, Brind didn't want to call out. He started to make his way along the streambed, searching, but had gone only twenty yards when he heard a voice: young, female, and cross.

"Will you please get me down!"

Looking up, Brind at first could see only a gray blur among the red and brown of the autumn trees. Then a tattered shoe hit him on the head. The shoe was Aurélie's, and so was the gray dress, suspended, with Aurélie inside it, high up in the treetops. Brind growled a quiet laugh. Fortunately, Aurélie didn't hear it.

Yesterday's rain had made the trunks and branches slippery, but the dog boy was nimble and strong and he loved climbing trees. Soon he was swaying close to Aurélie, far above the stream. Aurélie didn't like climbing trees, or the thought of falling out of them. She wanted to be on the ground, but she didn't want to move. She couldn't move anyway, because her dress was snagged on the branches.

"Knife?" requested Brind, holding out his hand.

But Aurélie had lost the kitchen knife when falling. Brind reached out, got hold of the hem of her dress with both hands, and ripped hard. The dress was caught in three places and he ripped three times. Aurélie was free but apparently not grateful.

"Clumsy!" she cried, clinging tighter to her branch.

Brind held out his hand again and jerked his head.

"Down now," he said.

Aurélie shook her head vehemently. Then an

unseen crow spoke so harshly and so close that it startled her into moving. Brind seized her hand and elbow and half pulled, half guided her down through the branches. Eventually, inevitably, they fell, but only onto a slope of soft, recently slipped earth, down which they rolled to the stream's edge. Aurélie tested herself for broken bones, then sat up.

"Thank you," she said. But her sarcasm was lost on Brind.

Then, remembering, she looked at the dog boy, her words quick and anxious.

"You still have the brooch?"

Brind produced the brooch and held it out to her.

"It was my father's," said Aurélie. "He was killed at Crécy."

The dog boy said nothing, but the sudden sadness in his eyes softened Aurélie's hard little heart. She pushed the brooch back at him.

"You look after it, please," she said. "I shall only lose it, like I lost the knife."

She pulled on her shoe, stood up, and violently brushed wet earth from her torn dress—a pointless exercise, but it meant she didn't have to look at Brind while her eyes filled. With a sniff, she looked around hopelessly at the seemingly endless ravine.

"What now?" she asked.

She should have known the answer.

"Find Glaive," said the dog boy.

One end of the hidden ravine was not far from Crécy. It was, in fact, the reason why Brind had lost Glaive's scent all those days ago. For Glaive, like Brind and Aurélie, had fallen. Senses dulled, body injured and weak, the lost dog had missed his footing and slithered over the unseen edge. He'd managed to scramble out of the stream at the bottom and limp to the shelter of a small cave of collapsed cliff and boulders. There he had sunk to the ground, exhausted; his body, voice, and scent all unintentionally hidden from the searching Brind.

But now Brind was less than a hundred yards away, although he didn't know it. He and Aurélie were picking their way along the rocky stream, still glancing up anxiously at the top of the ravine in case Sir Richard and his men should return.

Aurélie felt like a small beetle, totally exposed, crawling along a crack in a fallen tree trunk, expecting a bird or a fox to pounce and snap it up at any moment. She wished she was back in the dark forest that she hated. She wished also that they could find Glaive. For Brind's sake. That wish annoyed her: wanting something good for the coward English dog boy. She wasn't sure about the coward part anymore: Brind had risked everything to help her escape, and now was no better off than she was again. But he was still English; and he still looked and smelled like a dog.

Aurélie watched Brind stop in front of her for the hundredth time, raising his head, listening, sniffing. She wanted to give him a shove in the back. It was obvious they'd find nothing, dog or French army, until they were out of this stupid slit in the earth. Why didn't he just get on and find a way out? Brind had ceased moving his head and was standing quite, quite still. Suddenly, he ran away from Aurélie.

Slipping and splashing urgently between the rocks, then across a tiny beach, Brind was heading for the trees and ravine face beyond. Assuming that he'd been spotted and was running for cover, Aurélie stumbled after him.

There was a gap in the fallen boulders and earth at the foot of the ravine face, a kind of sagging cave, but instead of disappearing inside, Brind had fallen to his knees at the entrance and was still clearly visible. Fearfully, Aurélie looked over her shoulder and up at the tree-fringed top of the ravine, but could see nobody.

Brind was crouched now, making strange, quiet noises, and, as she approached more slowly, Aurélie realized: he must have found his precious dog.

It wasn't the kind of reunion Aurélie had expected, with lots of leaping up and licking and patting and barks of delight on both sides. But when she crouched behind Brind and peered over his shoulder, she saw why, and was shocked.

The dog had been large and powerful once but now was skin and bone. Its neck had shrunk within its collar, which had wicked-looking iron spikes on it. Even in the dim daylight that reached into the cave, Aurélie could see the dog's ribs through its skin. At first she thought it was dead, it lay so still and its eyes were so dull, but, as Brind stroked its ears, its tail twitched slightly. The horrible open wound, a great gash from neck to haunch, looked like raw meat, and, like raw meat, had attracted a thousand flies. Aurélie could smell the wound: it was festering, rotten. She had to turn away or be sick.

Feeling useless, almost an intruder, she ran to the stream and scooped up some water in her cupped hands. By the time she was back beside Brind there was no water left, but the dog, without lifting its head from the ground, licked feebly at her wet hands and Brind nodded his thanks to her.

Aurélie ran to the stream again and again. She got better at retaining the water in her hands and each time the dog licked them dry. All the while, Brind remained on his knees, stroking the dog, swatting away the flies, his voice a soft, soothing, rhythmic growl. He didn't seem affected by the stink of the wound, but nor did he attempt to move the dog. He smiled at Aurélie, though, when the tail began to beat faster, after her fifth visit to the stream.

At length, Brind evidently decided it was time to do something more for Glaive, but because the cave was low and small it was difficult for him to move the dog gently on his own. He unfastened and removed the iron collar, then indicated for Aurélie to put her hands under Glaive's head, and between them they very slowly eased the dog out into the fresh air.

The bright sunshine seemed to bother Glaive and he looked even worse out of the shadows. His coat was manged, the end of his tail was hairless. And there were maggots.

Aurélie steeled herself. Brind wanted to examine the dog's other side, which meant her getting close to the wound. She held her breath and lifted the legs as instructed. Glaive squealed but it was a pitiful, weak sound and he lay still on his back, teeth showing but eyes still vacant, as Brind peered at and felt along the previously hidden flank. To Aurélie's relief it seemed undamaged, and, to her even greater relief, Brind apparently agreed, and nodded for her to lower Glaive's legs. She did so as gently as she could, then turned away and allowed herself to breathe.

Brind moved from the dog and pulled handfuls of the grass that grew pale and tender in the nearby shade, then crouched again and used the grass gently but firmly to clean the wound. Aurélie couldn't watch and was glad when Brind gave her an instruction.

"Find betony," he said.

"Betony?"

Brind nodded. "Find betony."

But Aurélie didn't have a clue what he was talking about and could only stand, helpless and uncomfortable, until Brind had finished what he was doing and straightened up. He didn't appear angry or impatient with her.

"Betony," he said again, and moved off along the ravine, obviously searching.

Aurélie followed.

At last Brind found what he was looking for in a patch of cool, damp shade at the water's edge: a clump of purple-flowering plants. Brind picked them all.

"Betony," he grinned, in case Aurélie was still in doubt.

When he was back with Glaive, Brind tore the betony into pieces and repeatedly spat on them, crushing and mixing the resultant mess of plant and saliva in his hands until it was a crude kind of paste. Then he spread it along the wound, delicately pressing it in between the raw edges until nothing was visible of the red ugliness beneath. When he had finished, Brind looked up at Aurélie.

"Keep tight," he said, rotating his sticky green hands.

Aurélie understood this time: the treated wound needed to be bound up. But with what? Brind reached out with one of his sticky green hands and tugged gently at the hem of Aurélie's dress. Aurélie reacted slightly, then shrugged and took herself off behind a rock for a little privacy.

The dress was already torn from her adventure in the tree, but she still winced at the sound as she ripped further. The resultant strips had to be tied together to reach around Glaive's body, but they were wide enough to cover and close the wound and Brind looked happy as he tied the last knot.

Glaive remained indifferent, but he perked up when Brind delved inside his tunic and produced a greasy cloth bag. Aurélie wondered what else the curious dog boy kept in that tunic; she almost expected him to pull out a rabbit. In fact, from the greasy bag he emptied scraps of bread and chicken, cooked by Aurélie the night before and still almost good enough to eat.

The dog was fed first, and though the effort of eating quickly exhausted him, Glaive was clearly ravenous and continued to lick his lips appreciatively long after his head had dropped back to earth and he'd drifted off to sleep. Brind shared some of the remaining food with Aurélie, but put the rest back into the greasy bag.

Aurélie pondered on how long they might be staying on this tiny beach at the bottom of a ravine. It was obvious that Glaive couldn't be moved; and Brind wouldn't move without him. She imagined the French army marching farther and farther away from her.

In fact, it took a week. And by the end of it, with Glaive on his feet, able to walk and even bark, Aurélie was secretly sorry to have to move. Her restlessness had gone; revenge had become futile; she felt safe. The future was not safe; it was uncertain. But it was currently out of sight beyond the ravine and Aurélie preferred it that way. She had learned to climb trees; she had learned to catch fish with her hands; she had torn off the remainder of the bottom of her dress so what was left was more like a tunic, which let her legs breathe and enabled her to run and clamber as freely as the dog boy. She had even tended Glaive's wound, hunting for fresh betony and crushing and mixing it in her own hands before laying it gingerly along the uncomplaining dog's flank.

Brind had spent almost one whole day trying to light a fire, using different stones to strike against the iron of the spiked collar. When one had eventually struck sparks and the small pile of twigs and leaves had smoldered and flared, Aurélie had clapped in delight. And their first evening by the fire, with the fish cooking and Glaive sitting up, alert and licking Aurélie's hand, had been almost magical. True, she was getting a little tired of fish — it was all they had to eat now and the fish were small and bony. But Aurélie thought she could live with that; she could live here for a long time yet.

Brind was less content, though. Aurélie could see that. He never spoke much, but in the evenings, staring into the fire, he became completely silent. Aurélie supposed he must be dreaming of home. It upset her that she had no home to dream of. This tiny beach, with its cave and fire, dog and dog boy, was the best she could hope for. She forced herself to imagine what it would be like to say good-bye to Brind, and had to bite her lip hard to stop herself from crying.

But when the fateful morning arrived, when Glaive's wound had healed enough to be left uncovered, and the dog was strong enough to make his own way along the rocky ravine, Aurélie was composed.

"Go now," said Brind.

"About time, too," replied Aurélie, and she marched off ahead of him.

Brind had to hurry to keep up, and so did Glaive, and in his haste Brind forgot to stamp out the fire. It wasn't much of a fire—just a wisp of fragrant white smoke, rising from the ravine—but somebody saw it and reined in his horse.

Heavy boots came clattering and sliding onto the tiny beach, their owner having avalanched down through the thin trees in a shower of earth and stones. Shrewd, hard eyes took in the small heap of fish bones. A leather-gloved hand picked up the circle of spiked iron, still warm and white with ash, that had been used to contain the fire; and the shrewd, hard eyes considered it. Nostrils beneath the eyes sniffed the small cave and discerned the smell of dog. And dog boy. That was when the lips parted in a smile that could belong only to Tullo.

VI

THE PRISONER

"**H**igher!" cried the Frenchman. "Hold your wrist higher. Whisper to her. If she feels loved, she will relax."

Sir Edmund didn't care if the damned bird felt loved or not. But its claws had been digging into his gloved hand for half an hour now and he certainly wanted it to relax and fly away. His raised arm, his poor, battered old shield arm, was creaking with fatigue.

"Whisper in her ear!" The Frenchman laughed. "Pretend she's your wife."

The joke cut through Sir Edmund, though he

knew it wasn't meant to. The Frenchman wasn't ill-natured. It would have been so much easier if he were.

Sir Edmund tried to think of something to say to the falcon. He felt foolish, whispering to a bird, and he didn't like the feel of its feathers against his face. In the end the only word that came out was, indeed, the name of his wife.

"Beatrice . . . Beatrice . . ."

The bird's grip on his fist loosened.

"Now take off the hood," called the Frenchman. "Gently!"

Sir Edmund was still thinking of his wife and Dowe Manor, and everything that should have been and wasn't, but he removed the hood from the falcon's head. The bird seemed to glare hungrily at him with its fierce, unpleasant eyes, as if he himself were possible prey.

"The jesses," cried the Frenchman. "Quickly. She's ready to go."

Sir Edmund managed to slip the leather straps from the bird's legs and helped it on its way with an awkward flick of his hand. The falcon flapped unhurriedly away, low across the grassy hillside, before climbing into the blue northern sky.

Sir Edmund had a sudden fancy that it was flying to England and would seek out the small manor beneath the downs, where Beatrice was waiting for news, and would settle on the fence beside the kennels and tell her that her husband was safe. And sorry. He jerked his horse around and rejoined the Frenchman. Captivity was turning him soft in the head.

The Frenchman's name was Lucien. Lucien de Peronne. He was a pleasant man, of about Sir Edmund's age and social standing, although he lived in a castle rather than a manor house. It was a very small castle—drafty, uncomfortable, and cold, even in early autumn—but Lucien was proud of it. He was a widower, without children, and Sir Edmund sometimes wondered if Lucien had gone to war purely in the hope of capturing an Englishman to keep him company and share his delight in hawks and falcons. He was watching his falcon intently now. The bird was a tiny dot, high above them. It hadn't gone to England.

An unsuspecting wood pigeon emerged from the nearby copse and the falcon circled silently down, then dived. Its small shadow fell briefly over its prey but the alarm came too late and the pigeon was sent tumbling to the ground in a flurry of beating wings, its neck broken. The falcon sheered away, stalled, then dropped gently to its feast. Sir Edmund could hear its beak ripping at the pigeon and was glad when Lucien, by offering the falcon an even tastier titbit from a bag at his waist, tempted it away from its prey and onto his fist.

One of Lucien's hounds, an overweight, ill-disciplined bunch to Sir Edmund's mind, picked up the pigeon and carried it carefully in its jaws. Pigeon for dinner again tonight, thought Sir Edmund. How he longed for English venison.

Very occasionally, Sir Edmund caught himself relaxing and almost enjoying his captivity. He saw nothing bizarre in the rules of chivalry, whereby men of rank tried to slaughter one another but then, once the battle was over, observed a code of courtesy which made a prisoner a privileged house guest, generously welcomed, entertained, and provided for. Such pleasant loss of freedom could last for months, even years, until such time as the prisoner's ransom was paid. Then he was released, with safe conduct home guaranteed; and captor and captive exchanged farewells in the cheerful hope that they would meet, and fight, again.

When he'd ridden away from Dowe Manor back in the spring, Sir Edmund's thoughts had been of taking a prisoner himself: of bringing back to England some highborn French knight who could be ransomed for a chestful of gold. That would have pleased Beatrice; made everything all right. And he would have treated his French captive as graciously as Lucien was treating him. But it had not happened that way. Kill or be killed; kill or be captured. Sir Edmund was lucky to be alive, but even now he could hardly believe that everything had gone so wrong so quickly. He surprised himself with the depth of the bitterness he felt against Brind.

From Lucien's point of view, and he was far too well bred to hurt his prisoner's feelings by telling him so, Sir Edmund was a bit of a disappointment. A decent fellow, for an Englishman, and good company, when he was in the mood, though he seemed to have a blind spot where the joys of hawking were concerned; but he wasn't rich.

In the heat of battle, when he'd reared over the knight with the huge, brightly painted shield, Lucien had assumed he'd been confronted by an English champion, so far in front of the battle line had the man advanced. So instead of following up his first sword blow with a killing thrust, he'd scrambled off his horse, put his sword point to the champion's throat and demanded that he yield. The dazed Englishman had mumbled that he did yield and that he was Sir Edmund Dowe, whose liege lord was the Earl of Arundel. This had been confirmed by the knight's rather puny-looking page, who had come running from the battle line. Lucien had never heard of Sir Edmund Dowe but he had heard of the Earl of Arundel. It was only much later, having taken knight and page back to his castle, that he'd learned that the connection was remote and that the earl would be very unlikely to pay for Sir Edmund's release.

Lucien had toyed with the idea of releasing his prisoner without ransom, but decided this would be discourteous and wrong: Sir Edmund might feel insulted. And, after all, Lucien was one of the few French knights to have come out of the disastrous defeat at Crécy with anything at all to show for it. Sir Edmund might not be much, but he would have to be made the most of.

While Sir Edmund discreetly picked pigeon bones from his teeth, Lucien poured him another cup of wine and prepared to broach the subject.

"My dear friend," he said, "I have a proposal. In respect of your ransom."

Sir Edmund looked at him cautiously.

"I've told you how little I'm worth," he said.

"You are worth much." Lucien smiled. "You just happen to have little."

Sir Edmund shrugged at the compliment.

"And I have no wish to leave you with even less," continued Lucien. "To turn you and yours into paupers."

He sat back and paused.

"So I will settle for your dogs."

Sir Edmund frowned at him in surprise.

"My dogs are dead."

Even now he found it hard to say the words. Lucien quickly shook his head.

"No, no." He smiled. "Your dogs at home. The forty bitches. You say they are the finest in all of England. Well, I shall breed them with my own hounds and build the finest pack in all of France. Reason for us both to be proud, yes?"

The suggestion startled Sir Edmund. He sipped his wine, considering the implications. He had a vague feeling it might be treason on his part, a betrayal of England, to help create the finest pack of hounds in France. But perhaps that was being oversensitive. He also imagined, bleakly, what it would be like finally to arrive home and be greeted by the empty kennels. His only achievement would have been to get half his pack killed and then the other half given away to a Frenchman. There would be literally nothing left. The bare silence of the kennels would symbolize his total failure.

Sir Edmund put down his wine. No point in wallowing in misery. He would be alive, he would be free, and Beatrice would be there. He nodded courteously at Lucien.

"Very well," Sir Edmund said, his head held high.

So next morning Philip set off for England. It would have been possible, under the rules of chivalry, for Sir Edmund himself to have gone, on parole, with the solemn promise of returning to his captor with the agreed ransom. But Lucien preferred to keep his new companion with him in France.

Philip nodded respectfully as he was given interminable directions, instructions, and warnings, first by Lucien, then by Sir Edmund. Neither of them seemed to think him capable of finding his way out of the castle, let alone to Dowe Manor via Calais.

At last, though, they let him loose, and he felt suddenly exhilarated as he clattered away on the fine, strong chestnut mare Lucien had lent him. Philip was almost fourteen and for the first time in his life there was no rigid structure to the days ahead. Even on campaign there had been chores and lessons. And at Peronne it had been worse still, because there he'd found himself with two masters instead of one. But now there was nobody to nag or belittle him. He had his horse and his wits to keep him alive; and he had a mission. He sang out loud and was delighted to realize his voice was breaking. He was becoming a man.

Tullo could see the dog boy now. There was a girl with him; and a dog. Glaive. Tullo had his plans and they didn't include Brind. That is, they didn't include a Brind who wasn't dead.

Tullo was not a simple man but his plans were

plain and ruthless. He had seen both Hatton and Sir Edmund cut down by the French horsemen. After the battle, he'd found Hatton's body, though not Sir Edmund's. But it had been dark by then and he'd become bored with searching. He didn't want the responsibility of his ex-master's corpse anyway. By the time the English army had buried its dead and marched on toward Calais, Tullo had removed himself.

There had been no sign of Philip. Probably he'd run away, like the dog boy. Philip wouldn't dare return to England as a deserter, even if he knew how to get there. The useless ninny wouldn't survive anyway; he would starve or be skewered by the French. Tullo had nothing to fear from Philip. The dog boy was different.

The dog boy was a survivor, and Tullo wasn't quite sure how Lady Beatrice would react should Brind somehow find his way home. That was why Tullo had been looking for him: it was prudent to deal with the dog boy. Tullo nudged his horse forward, being careful to stay downwind.

✦ ✦ ✦

When the ravine opened up and the stream contin-ued on its way through pleasant open country, Aurélie took full credit.

"There, you see," she said, turning to Brind and spreading her arms as if she had created this new landscape. "Just follow me and you're fine."

Brind didn't congratulate her. He gazed around and glanced at the sun, then turned toward what he guessed to be north. Glaive took a brief drink at the stream, then padded after him. Aurélie ran past Glaive and walked beside Brind. She had no intention of becoming part of the pack.

Now that he was loping along with Glaive at his heel, Brind felt much happier. The dog would have the long, ugly scar forever, and always it would remind Brind of those terrible moments and terrible sounds on the hillside at Crécy. But that time was over. Glaive had been restored to him. The sense of loss and loneliness was gone. And how pleased the master would be when he, too, was reunited with his finest mastiff!

Brind imagined the broad smile of relief and delight on Sir Edmund's face when Glaive appeared before him, and the thought made him grin, too.

"What are you laughing at?" Aurélie's voice was sharply suspicious.

"Master," chuckled Brind, and he ran, just for the pleasure of running, and Glaive bounded after him, barking.

Both Philip and Tullo heard Glaive's voice. To Philip it meant nothing, other than that a dog wasn't far away, which might mean Frenchmen weren't far away either. He had a letter of safe conduct from Lucien, should he meet any groups of French knights; but he knew it would do him no good if he ran into one of the ragtag groups of rough soldiers now roaming the countryside. They tended to be less chivalrous and couldn't read. Philip turned his horse away from the sound of the dog. Tullo, meanwhile, paused, listening, then did the opposite.

It was more difficult to follow without being seen now the dog boy was in open country, but as long as Glaive barked now and then, Tullo would know where the little group was. He would be able to find them when they stopped for the night. Ideally, he would dispose of Brind but take the dog: Glaive would have a job to do back in England. The girl, who presumably was French, was of no interest and could be ignored, unless she made a nuisance of herself.

It was back to berries and mushrooms that evening. No fire, so they ate the mushrooms raw. And no honeycomb. Glaive wasn't very keen on mushrooms. While Brind and Aurélie sat munching in silence, the dog snuffled about in the leaf mold and managed to find a few grubs. He didn't seem to like the taste of these much either, but at least Aurélie was entertained as Glaive sniffed and barked at his wriggling supper, as if daring the grubs to make a run for it. Aurélie was rather disappointed that they simply twitched and accepted their fate.

There had been some daylight still left when they'd stopped. But having found Glaive and nursed him back from near death, Brind was being careful not to overtire him, so had called a halt early.

And they were back in the forest. Aurélie had pulled a face when Brind first headed into the trees, away from the sunlit hills, but she hadn't argued: Brind had a sense of purpose, and at present, she had none.

Quite how Brind intended to fulfill his purpose wasn't clear, either to Aurélie or, in fact, to Brind himself. He was intent on finding his master and seemed certain that by heading north he would do so, eventually.

Aurélie thought there was probably some sense in this: Calais was somewhere to the north, and if Brind's master was with the English army, that was where he would be. With the other locust pigs with their tents and flags and moldy bread. She'd managed not to think about any of that, or her mother, for several days; but if they were heading for

Calais, she would have to start thinking about it again soon. Aurélie wished they were back in the ravine.

Tullo dismounted quietly and tethered his horse to a tree. He was close now. He could hear the mastiff snuffling and yapping, and Brind laughing that strange laugh that was almost a bark. He could picture Brind rolling about in playful fight, spoiling the dog like he'd always done. That was the only problem: the dog. Tullo didn't want to kill it but he knew it would defend Brind to the death. He lifted the coiled whip from his saddle bow and crept forward.

Aurélie was first to see the demon. She screamed but it was too late. It burst from the undergrowth and sprang at the tangle of legs and heads that was Brind and Glaive, with its long tail lashing. It was much larger than the forest demons of her nightmares and Aurélie was petrified.

Brind and Glaive both scrabbled to their feet

in response to Aurélie's scream, and the familiar crack of the whip, but Tullo was already among them, seizing Brind and kicking Glaive violently away. The dog yelped, recovered, and made to spring back, but the whip lashed cruelly across his muzzle, bringing instant memories of punishment, pain, and subservience. Glaive glowered and snarled but stayed where he was, flinching as the whip cracked again, close above his scar.

Tullo threw Brind to the ground, stepped on him and drew his hunting knife, and Aurélie realized they'd been set upon not by a forest demon but by a man intent on murder. She launched herself at Tullo but he swayed aside and kicked her toward Glaive as if she were no more than a bundle of rags. She landed heavily against the dog and felt the rush of wind as the whip cracked inches from her face. Aurélie screamed again, more in helpless rage now than in fear.

Philip hadn't been mistaken: it was a scream. And there was another. A girl? Out here, miles from any village or farm? Philip wasn't lost exactly, but he'd gone too far out of his way earlier to avoid the barking dog, and had spent most of the afternoon trying to refind the track Lucien had set him on. The screams were none of his business; if he hadn't made his detour, he wouldn't have heard them anyway. But he didn't feel happy with that excuse. He was a page who hoped to become a squire and eventually a knight. He couldn't just pass by; it wouldn't be chivalrous. He spurred his horse into the trees.

Tullo was dragging Brind to his feet again. He had to keep his eyes on the dog, keep it subdued, while he finished the business. If he turned his back, even for a second, it would be on him. He cracked the whip again and was genuinely astonished when the action seemed to produce, from nowhere, a horse. He was even more astonished when he recognized the pimply streak of pond water on its back.

Philip's horse reared and backed away from the whip and the crouching, angry dog. Calming it gave Philip a moment to recover from his own surprise. He recognized Brind. And he recognized Sir Edmund's huntsman. Philip had always been afraid of Tullo. The man's insinuated but obvious contempt had made him feel weak and ineffectual. But that was when Philip was a boy. He was a man now. He jumped from the saddle with unexpected agility and drew his sword.

"Let the boy go!" he demanded.

Tullo laughed, the contempt now quite unrestrained. There were no rules here, no need for feudal respect; strength and cunning were all that mattered. But he was startled enough to lose his grip on Brind when Philip charged at him without another word and hacked through the leather shoulder of his jerkin.

Philip's heart was beating fast; he could hear and feel it. That was the first time he'd struck a man in anger. At Crécy he'd been told by Sir Edmund to stay back while he and the mastiffs marched forth. When Sir Edmund had fallen, Philip had rushed to him, only to be met with politeness from the victorious

French knight. And, with the knight, he had helped Sir Edmund from the battlefield. Now, suddenly, Philip was in single combat.

He tried to remember everything he'd learned during his six wearisome years of instruction and implied failure, but all he could think of was to swing his sword and knock the huntsman down. Tullo was wounded and wary now, but the hunting knife in his hand was long and sharp and real. And he still smiled. His eyes were fixed on Philip's. There was hate in the eyes, and finality. Kill or be killed.

Philip could feel the panic swelling inside him, so, with a shout, he ran at Tullo again, but his sword was knocked aside and Tullo pulled him close, and, with a deft, hard flick of the foot, brought him to the ground. Tullo was heavy, muscular, and savage, and his grunts were feral. It was like wrestling with a wild boar. Philip somehow knew the outcome. He no longer panicked. He had overcome fear; he had been chivalrous. He didn't even feel the boar's tusk.

When Tullo stood up, he was alone. Philip's horse was grazing nearby, oblivious to the death of its rider; but Brind, Glaive, and the girl had gone.

Tullo stalked into the undergrowth, one moment stealthy, the next slashing angrily at saplings and brambles. He searched for nearly half an hour but found no trace. When he returned to the clearing, the horse had gone, too.

Not until it was completely dark did Brind feel it safe to rest. He and Aurélie had hurried on into the deepest part of the forest—leading the horse rather than riding it, because the low, dense branches made being on horseback dangerous. Glaive panted along wearily behind them and collapsed the moment Brind and Aurélie finally halted. But neither Brind nor Aurélie could sleep: shock and fear kept them wide awake. Nor did they speak. Aurélie was still numb from what she had seen, and Brind was too perplexed. He was used to the malevolence and beatings, but why did Tullo now want to kill him? Surely not simply because Brind had bitten his wrist?

Then Brind remembered something else about that night after the great hunt: Tullo had called him a traitor. Was that it? Was that why Tullo was pursuing him? Was Brind a traitor? What was a traitor?

Aurélie could think only of the tall, skinny boy, lying still in the dirt when she and Brind had crept back to the clearing. Before that, they had hidden in the entrance to a badger sett, on a bank, beneath the exposed roots of an oak tree. It had been like crouching under the twisted fingers of a giant's hand; and the hand had protected them. Tullo had passed by no more than twenty yards away, but even Glaive had remained as still and quiet as the tree roots. Then they had slipped back to the clearing and Brind had squeezed Aurélie's hand hard to stop her crying out. He had whispered that the boy's name had been Philip and that he'd been page to his master. Aurélie couldn't look closely, but it was she who had the presence of mind to take the horse.

+ + +

Tullo searched the dead page methodically. You did it to the enemy, so why not your own side? There was nothing of value but Tullo was thorough. He didn't quite understand what Philip had been about. He'd been alive, for a start, which was a surprise; but then there'd been the horse. It wasn't one of Sir Edmund's, so whose was it, and how had Philip come to be prancing around northern France on it?

Then Tullo felt the packet, lightly stitched inside the fancy padded tunic. He quickly slit the fabric with his hunting knife and pulled out stuffing and a folded piece of parchment. He didn't recognize the wax seal but once he'd broken that and unfolded the parchment, the predatory smile slowly returned. Tullo knew his master's signature when he saw it.

"Traitor?"

Aurélie frowned. It was a strange question to be asked at dawn. Her neck and back were stiff as a result of having finally fallen asleep awkwardly against a tree trunk. She was hungry and thirsty, and trying not to think about the tall, skinny page. She struggled for a definition.

"A traitor is somebody who's disloyal. To his country or his king," she said at last. "Or to God," she added, because it sounded impressive.

Brind looked unenlightened.

"Disloyal," said Aurélie. "You know what that means? Not loyal. Not good. Not to be trusted. Bad."

Brind understood bad.

"Why are you asking?" said Aurélie, stretching her back and neck, and enviously watching the horse as it munched its way across a small patch of grass.

"Tullo said."

Aurélie knew who Tullo was by now.

"Tullo said what?" she asked warily.

"Traitor." Brind pointed at himself.

"Tullo said you're a traitor?" Aurélie was in the dark now. "Why?"

"Run after Glaive," said Brind.

He stroked the dog and shrugged unhappily.

Running after a dog didn't seem a treasonable offence to Aurélie, but then, Sir Richard Baret had referred to Brind as a coward and that didn't seem right either. Perhaps the English just had funny ideas about such things. But Brind still looked troubled. Aurélie felt she ought to make more of an effort. She knelt in front of the dog boy and took his hands. There was a fuzz of hair on their backs and that, and their long blackened nails, gave them a slight resemblance to paws, but Aurélie pretended not to notice.

"You're not a coward, Brind," she said, and meant it. "And you're not a traitor, either."

Brind held her look for a moment, then turned away.

"Find master," he said. As if only Sir Edmund could reassure him and put his world straight again.

Aurélie felt rejected. She stood up and turned to the horse, which seemed placid enough, tugging its saddlecloth straight and tightening its girth, for something to do. There was a small coat of arms embroidered on the saddlecloth and she saw it for the first time. Red falcons on a field of yellow. Aurélie stopped. Red falcons ... red falcons ... While she searched her memory, she unfastened the small saddlebag. Stupid. Why hadn't she noticed the saddlebag before? There could be food in it.

There was no food, only some silver, which was useless in the middle of a forest; and a small piece of parchment, so thin and smooth that at first Aurélie thought it was just a loose lining to the saddlebag. She took it out anyway. There was writing on it. Aurélie read the brief message once, twice, three times. A letter of safe conduct. She turned to a startled Brind, dancing up and down and waving the scrap of parchment in front of him.

"Lucien de Peronne!" she cried. "Brind, I know where your master is!"

Neither of them was to know that Tullo was already on his way.

VII

REUNIONS

There were just the two of them: Lucien and Sir Edmund. Lucien liked to leave his huntsmen, his servants, even his dogs behind on such trips. He liked to have nobody to care for or to be cared for by; to be a lone hunter, or two lone hunters, just living off the land. With the comfort of a splendid lodge to sleep in at night, of course.

The hunting lodge was very comfortable indeed. Timber-built, with a high roof, fine wall-hangings, fleeces, and furs everywhere, and a hearth wide enough to have stabled a horse. Above all, it was warm. Sir Edmund couldn't understand why

Lucien didn't live in it all the time, instead of his depressing, cold little castle.

A haunch of venison, blackened red and spiked with herbs, sizzled and spat above the flickering fire. It smelled wonderful, even though it looked no bigger than a rabbit in the glowing, cavernous space of the hearth; and Sir Edmund was starving. The pleasurable kind of starving that knows favorite food is on the way. He ached all over, but that was pleasant, too. He and Lucien had risen before dawn and charged around the countryside all day. For some reason, the war hadn't touched this small corner of northern France. Perhaps that would change, but in the meantime game was still plentiful and the hunting, like the weather, superb. And Sir Edmund himself had slain the stag with a single shot of his hunting bow. The honor of England had been upheld, and not a damned falcon in sight.

A good day in the field always raised Sir Edmund's spirits, and, since dispatching Philip to collect the unusual ransom, he had allowed himself to feel less guilty about his enjoyment. He had done all he could, including the long, reassuring and, he thought, elegantly affectionate letter to Beatrice. He was rather proud of the letter. If, by the spring, Philip hadn't returned with the mastiffs, Sir Edmund—and Lucien—would have to think again. But spring was a long way off. Sir Edmund could relax with a clear conscience.

Lucien snored close by, feet stretched toward the fire, drowsy with exercise and warmth. Sir Edmund would wake him when the meat was done, but he was quite content to sit with his own thoughts for company in the meantime. He relived the day's hunt: every hill, every stream, every copse and fallen tree. The great leap of his horse across the ruined wall . . . the calling of the hounds. They were calling still . . . Sir Edmund's dozing eyes opened abruptly. There had been no hounds on the hunt.

He stood up and listened, but could hear only the crackle and singing of the logs on the hearth. He glanced at Lucien, still snoring, his mouth hanging open unattractively. When Sir Edmund slept like that, Beatrice gave him a prod. Clearly, Lucien had heard nothing. Perhaps Sir Edmund had too. Imagination, then; or a wistful dream, slipping through his defenses, reminding him yet again of Glaive and the finest pack of mastiffs in all of England. Sir Edmund didn't want that dream. He paced a little before sitting down again, then instantly sprang up. There *was* something outside. He found his sword, marched to the door, paused, then threw the door open.

Glaive stood looking up at Sir Edmund, panting and swinging his tail. At least, the astonished knight thought it was Glaive: the hound was much thinner than he should be and disfigured by a great scar that glowed red in the sunset. Then the dog barked once, softly, and Sir Edmund was certain. Behind Glaive stood a ragged waif of a girl with a determined little face; and beside her stood Brind. There was no mistaking *him*: Brind, who had been nurtured and trusted; Brind, who had betrayed that trust so spectacularly; Brind, who had lost control of the pack and then simply run away.

Sir Edmund stared at the dog boy. He could see no trace of remorse; not a hint of repentance or self-reproach. Clearly, Brind hadn't reappeared in order to throw himself at his master's feet and apologize. In fact, he was grinning that doglike grin, showing the pointed teeth, and nodding at Glaive, as if he were pleased with himself.

Sir Edmund lost control. With a great cry of anguish, he slashed at Brind with his sword. He missed and Brind tumbled backward, as fearful and confused as Glaive, who had never seen Sir Edmund attack Brind in this way and didn't know how to respond, except by barking loudly. Sir Edmund stumbled after Brind, swinging the sword blindly. Once again Aurélie had cause to wonder at the extreme reactions the dog boy seemed to provoke in people.

"Stop, stop!"

Somebody was shouting behind them. Sir

Edmund was standing over Brind now, but suddenly he was barged aside by a slim, gray-haired man. Lucien de Peronne, thought Aurélie, noting his aristocratic French accent, and was delighted with herself for having found him. Sir Edmund threw his sword to the ground and walked away from Brind, his shoulders heaving. His back was turned, but Aurélie knew he was crying.

"Get up!" Lucien was speaking to Brind now. "Quieten the dog."

He seemed to understand who Brind and Glaive were. He should have done; he'd heard about them often enough from his captive guest. Aurélie decided it was time to speak. Brind was stunned by his hostile reception and she knew he didn't have the words to explain himself. She launched in.

"My lord," she cried.

She was addressing Lucien but also looking toward Sir Edmund, who was standing with his back still turned, gazing at the setting sun.

"This boy is no coward or traitor. He is brave:

he saved my life. He is loyal: he searched for and found his master's precious dog."

Aurélie didn't really understand how a mere dog could be precious, but that wasn't the point.

"He saved the dog's life, too, with great skill."

She smoothed Glaive's back, running her finger along the healing scar.

"And then his only thought was to return it to his master. It has been a long and dangerous journey, but he was determined to do his duty."

She paused.

"So here we are," she concluded, and felt it was a slightly lame finish, though she was pleased with the rest.

Whether or not Brind was pleased, she couldn't tell, but to her disappointment Sir Edmund didn't turn and embrace the dog boy with smiles of understanding and gratitude. He didn't turn at all. And Lucien merely looked at her suspiciously.

"How did you find us?" He frowned.

"We went to your castle," said Aurélie. "And were directed from there."

Lucien's look grew even darker.

"But how did you know to go to my castle?"

"Lucien."

Sir Edmund's voice was flat. He wasn't gazing at the beautiful purple sunset after all, but at a chestnut mare, tethered in the trees.

"They have Philip's horse."

Tullo was in too deep to stop now. He'd been rocked when he'd realized Sir Edmund wasn't dead after all; but only for a second. Because the letter he'd ripped from Philip's tunic had told him everything he could want to know, even though he'd understood only one word in ten. Philip now wouldn't be delivering the letter to Lady Beatrice, or returning with the ransom, but Tullo kept the letter anyway. It might be useful when he himself got back to England. Crucially, the letter told him where to find the irritatingly still alive Sir Edmund.

As Tullo rode toward Peronne, he had no trouble convincing himself that Sir Edmund actually deserved to die. Getting killed at Crécy would have been the decent thing. Instead, he was languishing in comfortable captivity. Where was the honor in that? Death was glory, wasn't it, to chivalrous knights? Even fat, foolish ones like Sir Edmund. Tullo would be doing him a favor.

There was still the problem of the dog boy, but Sir Edmund had priority. First the master, then the servant. It was the proper order of things. Tullo smiled and dug in his spurs.

It took two days to reach Peronne, on unfamiliar roads, and when Tullo got there, the French were cagey. They'd already had one lot of inquiries about their lord and his English prisoner. When Tullo said he had urgent news of the ransom messenger, Philip, the French replied that the girl and boy with the dog had said the same—and they had with them the chestnut mare to prove it. In the end, Tullo grudgingly tossed some silver on the ground in exchange for information, and was directed to the hunting lodge. It was no great expense, really: he'd stolen the money from a dead Frenchman in the first place.

The hunting lodge was good news, despite the extra riding. Evidently it was isolated, and Sir Edmund and his French knight had gone there alone. If the dog boy was there as well now, that made the good news even better.

The moon was rising when Tullo finally arrived in sight of the lodge. He approached on foot for the last hundred yards, stealthy as a lynx. The pungent smells of wood smoke and roasting venison filled the air. If there were dogs around, they wouldn't scent him.

Tullo crouched and froze as a horse whinnied, out of sight behind the lodge. Then a figure, carrying a bucket, appeared around the corner from the direction of the sound and went into the lodge. Tullo recognized the silhouette and the loping walk. If he had been a dancing man, he would have danced for joy.

✦ ✦ ✦

Brind put the bucket of water on the earthen floor and Glaive lapped at it gratefully. Both dog and boy found the hunting lodge unbearably hot. Neither of them ever came into the great hall at Dowe Manor and they were unused to being indoors with a fire. Glaive lay down as far from the flames as possible. Brind squatted beside him and ate charred venison. He'd been given only the burnt bits but he didn't care: it was meat and he gorged himself.

Aurélie was still talking to Sir Edmund and the French knight. She'd been allowed to sit on a chair. She was talking quickly and Brind had given up trying to understand what she or the masters said. He was still recovering from the shock of being attacked by Sir Edmund. He realized that Aurélie had spoken for him. He also realized that the news of Philip's death had affected Sir Edmund deeply. But Brind was confused and upset by the violent reception he'd received. And deeply disappointed by his master's lack of interest in Glaive. Sir Edmund hadn't patted or stroked or even spoken to his favorite hound all evening. The mastiff had been completely ignored.

Brind made up for this neglect, growling affection in the great dog's ear, and consoled himself with the thought that at least dog, boy, and master had been reunited. Brind could eat and sleep and wait to be told what to do next. No more finding.

Aurélie had told the two knights her own story, or most of it: she'd said she'd become separated from her mother outside Calais, rather than having left a note and run away. And, in deference to Sir Edmund, she didn't refer to the English as locust pigs. Otherwise, she gave an accurate account of what had happened to her and Brind; repeatedly underlining the dog boy's bravery, skill, and sense of duty to such a degree that in the end Sir Edmund raised his hand and gave her a pained look.

Aurélie had better hopes of her future now. Lucien de Peronne seemed kind. He was sympathetic about the death of her father and certain that he must have died bravely. Aurélie wondered if Lucien might offer her permanent shelter, employment, even patronage. If so, and she and Brind had to part company, she would have repaid any debt she might owe the dog boy. She had guided him here and she had defended him. The rest was up to him.

Aurélie did say a little too much on the respective merits of the French and English armies, telling Sir Edmund that French knights on horseback were so skilled and disciplined, and rode so close together, that if you threw a plum at them it inevitably would be impaled on a lance. A French cavalry charge, she informed Sir Edmund, was like a hedgehog of death: nothing could get past the spines.

Sir Edmund looked diplomatically at the floor, and Lucien said mildly that, actually, it hadn't been quite like that at Crécy. Aurélie blamed the cowardly Genoese crossbowmen for that, but Lucien just shrugged. And when Aurélie said it certainly wouldn't be long before the French king rallied his troops and broke the siege of Calais, he shrugged again.

"Who can tell?" he said sadly.

After that, Aurélie thought it wiser to hold her tongue. When she received a nod from Lucien, she curtsied politely and sought out Brind and Glaive in the darkest, coolest corner. She lay for a while, gazing up at the fire shadows dancing under the roof, then, like the dog boy and the mastiff, she was lulled to sleep by the serious murmur of conversation from the two knights still sitting by the hearth.

Lucien eventually left Sir Edmund and went to his bracken bed. He patted his prisoner friend's shoulder comfortingly as he went, appreciating full well the impact of events.

The death of his page had brought an abrupt end to Sir Edmund's comfort. He could no longer relax until the spring. He didn't exactly feel guilty about Philip, but the boy had died in his service; killed, moreover, by another of Sir Edmund's own servants. However it had happened, whatever Tullo's motives, action was required—but what action? How was he to find Tullo? And what about the ransom now? And Beatrice?

Sir Edmund clutched at the remote possibility that Tullo's intentions were proper: that he had tracked down Brind to punish him for his supposed cowardice; that Philip had blundered in and stupidly provoked a fight; and that Tullo was now on his way to England to make everything right with his master by completing the mission and bringing back the mastiffs. But even Sir Edmund couldn't believe all of that.

He wouldn't have been able to believe the truth either: that Tullo was lying just fifty yards away, waiting to kill him.

The door of the lodge opened and a fullish figure emerged. It wandered about a little, taking deep breaths of cool night air, then went back in.

Tullo heard the wooden latch close behind Sir Edmund and imagined those inside settling down to sleep. He especially imagined Brind and Sir Edmund. He couldn't smell venison anymore, so they must have eaten it all. He would be sending them to hell on a full stomach; they should be grateful for that.

Tullo supposed *he* would go to hell eventually. The thought didn't perturb him: he would be as ready to curse and fight with the Devil as he was with everyone else. And once tonight was over he had plenty of time left on earth. More especially, he had plenty of time left at Dowe Manor, where he would be, to all intents and purposes, the master. But there was no hurry. The deeper into sleep they all were, the better. The timber-built lodge, with its internal glow and occasional drifts of smoke, reminded Tullo of a smoldering bonfire. Or a funeral pyre.

When at last he decided the time was right, Tullo moved with the quiet certainty of any night predator. There were no sentries, which made things easy but angered him briefly: he felt slighted that Sir Edmund didn't appear to comprehend him as a threat. Surely Brind and the girl had warned the old fool? No matter. Tullo gathered kindling and tinder from the wood store next to the stable and arranged it carefully. The sharp, clean smell of resin in the pine logs of the lodge wall pleased him. Then he returned to the thicket where he had left his horse. From his saddle-bow he lifted the small earthenware pot that he always took with him on long hunts. The embers inside were still warm.

It was the noise that woke Brind rather than the intense heat. A creaking, tearing noise and then a crash. The crash woke everyone except Lucien de Peronne, who was killed by the falling beam that caused it. All around Brind were walls of flame and the roof above him burned too; but the flames consumed the air he should have breathed and already Brind was too suffocated to panic.

Glaive also was stupefied. He moved his tail, lurched to his feet, then collapsed, looking help-lessly at Brind. Further away, Sir Edmund was on his knees, head down, like a sick animal.

Only Aurélie was upright. She was shouting at Brind, but he couldn't hear what she said because she held a handful of bracken over her mouth. She plucked at Brind's arm and pointed, then removed the bracken and yelled in his ear as she pulled at him.

"The hearth!"

Aurélie had been trapped in a house fire before.

Brind felt sick and his legs seemed detached, but he managed to get up and haul Glaive with him across the scorched earthen floor; over the fleeces and furs that were blazing and shriveling to nothing.

Another roof beam hit the ground where they'd been lying, disintegrating in red-hot wafers. Then water hit Brind in the face, thrown by Aurélie from the bucket Brind had brought in for Glaive earlier. Aurélie was already wet, her hair and tattered dress steaming. She splashed Glaive, then threw the remains of the water over Sir Edmund. Clearly there was no point in wasting it on Lucien.

Brind understood now about the hearth: it was built of stone; it was the only part of the lodge that wouldn't burn. He shoved Glaive into the hot, black cavern, then, with Aurélie's help, dragged Sir Edmund, who was unconscious from lack of air, in too. And there they cowered, their feet blistered and with wet bracken pressed to their faces, while the fire storm raged in front of them.

Tullo watched the fire from horseback, ready to ride down any fleeing survivors, but none emerged; only a few rats, and charitably he let those pass. When the remains of the roof finally fell in, with a satisfying mushroom cloud of flame and flying sparks, Tullo rode off, taking the horses from the stable with him.

"French fire traps," tutted Sir Edmund, shaking his head disparagingly. "French fire traps. Not like good English houses."

It was all he could say; all he had been saying since dawn, when the three blackened humans and their dog had finally emerged from their sanctuary. As if it had been waiting for them to leave, the hearth, and the rough stone chimney above it, collapsed in a heap behind them, sending up a billow of hot dry ash as fine as dust.

Brind felt singed, baked hard. Like one of the loaves that Milda often forgot in the kitchen at Dowe Manor and pulled hastily from the oven to cool. Brind was cool now, but he would never again be able to eat Milda's bread without thinking of the night just past. A roaring, red night of heat so intense it had burnt away his eyebrows and the hair on the backs of his hands.

But now the fire was spent; and so was Sir Edmund. He slumped on the dewy grass, staring, red-eyed, at the burned-out space and continuing to shake his head about French fire traps. Aurélie wondered if his mind had gone, like her grandfather's. Glaive seemed concerned too, and licked the knight's hands and face as if he were an overgrown puppy in need of care. Absently, Sir Edmund began to pat the dog. He frowned at the long scar, as if noticing it for the first time, but still he tutted. Only when Brind stood in front of him with the small earthenware pot did clarity and purpose return, sharply.

"Tullo," said Brind, handing him the pot.

But Sir Edmund had recognized it already.

Tullo had remembered the pot a couple of hours after leaving the lodge. When he stopped and turned in the saddle, he could see a red glow in the sky. The fire was still burning. He could picture where he'd left the pot of embers but decided not to waste time by going back. The pot wouldn't be incriminating: it would mean nothing to the Frenchman's people if eventually they came looking for their master. And in any case, Tullo would be back in England by then.

Sir Edmund threw handfuls of ash to the light morning breeze and murmured what he could remember of a prayer. It was the best he could do for Lucien. He had no means of taking him back to Peronne for burial; there was nothing to take anyway. But should he not go to Peronne to explain? And what would be the position, in chivalric terms, if he did? He was Lucien's prisoner but Lucien was dead. Sir Edmund wasn't sure if he was still a prisoner or not. After all, the agreed ransom hadn't been paid. But surely he couldn't make himself somebody else's prisoner instead? The bond was a personal one, with Lucien.

In the end, Sir Edmund decided that Lucien would have regarded the bond as severed by death; that it would not be dishonorable to regard himself as free.

He had a qualm about not returning to Peronne, if only to break the news to the household there, but it was a long way to walk, and in the opposite direction to Calais. He would write a letter when he could, but now they had to press on. Brind, Glaive, and the girl were ready to go. They looked young and strong and eager. It was an uncomfortable thought to Sir Edmund that he, their lord, might become a liability instead of a leader.

✦ ✦ ✦

At first, all went well enough. The track was firm and dry, the weather good, and Sir Edmund was traveling light. His great shield had been split asunder at Crécy and probably the bits were lying there still. And his sword had been warped into uselessness by the intense heat of last night's inferno. He was sad to leave the sword behind, but at least he didn't have to carry it. Instead, he cut a sapling to use as a staff, and imagined that he looked like a pedlar, or a friar, or, more likely, a vagrant, wandering the country with his odd, grimy family.

He glanced frequently at Brind. The dog boy loped beside him, respectfully matching his pace to that of his master, with Glaive panting along at heel. Every time Sir Edmund looked at Brind, the dog boy smiled in such a hopeful and trusting way that it almost broke Sir Edmund's heart. Despite everything he'd been put through, the dog boy was still blindly loyal to his master, and the master felt deeply unworthy. Sir Edmund just wanted to get home. He wanted it desperately. But the endless lanes of France stretched ahead, and Tullo's cruel, bitter face kept looming in front of him.

Aurélie walked in silence, an unusual state for her. She had got too excited yesterday at her sudden prospects. In fact, she had gone to sleep in the lodge composing a demure acceptance speech for when Lucien de Peronne invited her to come and live in his castle as his ward.

By morning there had been no Lucien, and no prospects. Aurélie was back to thinking about Calais, where, apparently, the English were not soon to be swept into the sea. And about her mother.

"Have you still got the brooch?" she asked Brind abruptly.

Brind looked at her, then delved inside his tunic, producing a few black lumps of venison that he'd saved from last night's feast, and then the brooch. He handed it to Aurélie, who made a show of wiping it clean, before, with difficulty, pinning it to her dress. Its weight caused the thin fabric to sag but she didn't care.

Brind nodded and grinned at her, but this irritated Aurélie and she walked on, rather haughtily. Suddenly it was important to her to be French and independent. The brooch was her coat of arms.

The accident happened on the third day. They were walking down a flinty slope when Sir Edmund's staff slipped on the hard, shiny stones, and he fell heavily, twisting his knee. He tried to rise quickly, as if nothing had happened, but the knee gave way and left him lying on the ground, cursing and helpless.

Brind found a stream and made a cold compress with a strip of Sir Edmund's own undershirt, but the knee continued to swell. There was no way Sir Edmund could walk. Probably not for several days. Brind and Aurélie helped him to the shade of a small wayside tree and propped him against it. Then Brind rinsed Tullo's earthenware pot, which he'd kept, and filled it with fresh water.

"Don't fuss," said Sir Edmund, becoming increasingly angry. "Don't fuss!"

And when Brind and Glaive settled down beside him, he flew into a rage.

"What are you getting comfortable for? Leave me! Leave me! Find Calais! Find the king! Find the earl!"

Brind received such a clout across the side of the head that his ears rang. So he did as he was told and left his master, cautiously giving him the remaining lumps of venison before he went.

Sir Edmund watched the trio dwindling along the track: the loping boy, the girl walking busily beside him, the dog padding along behind. Boy and dog turned several times, but Sir Edmund didn't acknowledge them.

Aurélie was glad to be free of Brind's master. She wished him no harm; he was gruff but not harsh. But he was so much less refined than Lucien de Peronne; and, although he spoke

French, he was English. She could see no future in him.

Brind was trying hard to remember what the Earl of Arundel looked like, or his coat of arms; he was also memorizing wayside landmarks so he could direct the earl, or whichever of his servants Brind was allowed to speak to, when they came to rescue Sir Edmund.

But then, after a few hours, Aurélie confused all that by plunging off the main track and onto the narrowest of paths through the trees. Brind tugged her arm and looked puzzled, but Aurélie didn't stop. She wanted to lead.

"This is a shortcut," she declared. "I know where I am now."

She sensed they were quite close to Calais, and this might have been one of the paths she'd traveled when she'd first run away. Then again, it might not. Either way, she and Brind and Glaive were far out of earshot when the troop of horsemen drummed by.

✦　✦　✦

Sir Edmund shifted uncomfortably and gnawed at the last of the venison. Better save the water: he could be here for days. He wished he still had his sword, bent and buckled though it was. He had his staff, but that wouldn't be much use against French cutthroats. Especially from a sitting position. He should have kept Glaive with him. But surely this was territory controlled by the English now? Even if Brind didn't find his way to Calais, a patrol would come by sooner or later and whisk Sir Edmund away to the coast.

A small cloud of dust to the north caught his attention. Dust or a fire? No, it was moving. Coming his way. Sir Edmund tried to straighten up, bracing his back against the tree and pushing with his good leg, but it was no use. He was too heavy. He lowered himself again, wincing at the pain, and sat with the staff across his lap. Waiting.

Eventually the horsemen came into view. A large group, about fifty of them; and in good order. French or English? Sir Edmund couldn't make out their flag until they were almost upon him and then his grip on the staff tightened. The horsemen weren't French. They were led by Sir Richard Baret.

VIII
CALAIS

The tall knight of the silver unicorns reined in his horse and gazed down at Sir Edmund. He never seemed surprised by anything.

"Last week the boy," he said, smiling. "This week the master."

Sir Edmund had always felt deficient in the presence of Sir Richard. Now, lying in the dirt, sooty, swordless, and immobile, he felt humiliated.

"And not dead, Sir Edmund. Splendid."

Sir Richard dismounted gracefully.

"No," said Sir Edmund. "Not dead."

But what had Baret meant about the boy? Then

Sir Edmund remembered Aurélie's account of their meeting.

Sir Richard was crouching beside him now. He held the water pot to the stricken knight's lips, unnecessarily, as if to underline Sir Edmund's helplessness.

"Well, the boy *is* dead," said Sir Richard. "The dog boy."

He sounded only mildly sorry.

"Indeed?"

Sir Edmund had become crafty, but hoped he didn't sound it.

"Yes," said the tall knight. "He fell into a ravine not far from Crécy. Smashed his skull and drowned." He shrugged. "But no matter. He proved a disappointment to us all. Can you ride if we get you on a horse?"

Sir Edmund said he could, and Sir Richard's men, with some amusement, raised him up on a pack pony so short that Sir Edmund's feet dangled only inches from the ground. He clung to the rope halter as the pony jolted on its way, and felt the indignity cut deeper than the pain in his knee. He had been rescued and insulted in one act. It was Sir Richard's greatest talent.

The tall knight apologized for not taking Sir Edmund directly to Calais: he and his men must complete their patrol first. But he was sure the bold knight of Dowe could endure the discomfort for a few hours. Sir Edmund would be delivered safely to the English camp by nightfall.

It appeared that Sir Richard and his men were based with the besieging army now, but came out foraging every day. Sir Richard talked of returning to England soon. There was no glory, or even amusement, in sitting staring at the walls of Calais week in, week out. The war had ground to a halt.

He was politely interested in Sir Edmund's capture and his fortuitous escape from the fire. Sir Edmund kept his wits and said nothing about Tullo being the culprit, or Brind being alive. Tullo was Sir Edmund's own business. He didn't want to ask for Sir Richard's help in tracking him down. At the moment, Sir Edmund was completely in the tall knight's power. It would be even worse to be in his debt. Brind, he knew, would be the price; and he had no intention of paying it.

Aurélie was amazed when the forest suddenly thinned and the low, marshy lands around Calais lay spread out before them. The walled town itself was no more than three miles away. Her shortcut had actually worked.

"Calais," she said simply, and sat down to rest.

Brind remained standing, looking toward the town and the sea beyond. He sniffed the air and caught the tang of salt and seaweed. Glaive, panting beside him, glanced at Brind, then followed his example, raising his head to the distant mauve horizon. The slight wind from the sea lifted the dog's ears and smoothed the hair along his back, either side of the scar, which always looked worse in the evening sun.

Boy and dog stood quite still, each in his own way sensing the nearness of home. Before being brought to France, Brind had never needed an imagination. He had lived his life by sight and sound and scent. But the long months of hardship, terror, and adventure had brought his mind alive, and he pictured Dowe Manor now in its tiniest detail: from the female mastiffs milling in their feed yard, to the bracken on the kennel benches, to the fragile, pale spiders hanging on their webs beneath the low rafters.

But despite the deep longing, duty was paramount. Aurélie knew exactly what the dog boy was going to say when he'd finished staring and sniffing, and he didn't let her down.

"Find earl," he said, with that infuriating sense of purpose.

He was always finding something. Find Glaive, find betony, find master, now find earl. Aurélie was weary of finding. Now that she was back almost where she'd begun, she certainly didn't want to find her mother. Wrong as she'd been to run away in the first place, it was no use pretending. What would her return achieve? What could Aurélie do for her mother, in the half-life outside the town walls, besides beg or steal food, and be grateful to the taunting English for not killing them both?

Aurélie told herself again and again that she was selfish, but she couldn't subdue the need to do, to fight, to live. Suddenly she envied Brind once more, as she had done, misguidedly, that night at Sir Richard's camp, only more sharply still. She envied his companionship with the scarred dog, and she envied his simple hope: Brind had only to cross the sea now to be happy. Aurélie unpinned her father's brooch and pressed its cool weight hard against her cheek until her silent tears made it wet.

It was easy enough for Tullo to find a ship to take him back to England. The port of Calais was now in English control, so an endless stream of supply ships and even trading vessels plied back and forth across the Channel.

Tullo chose a small, rotund craft that smelled of sheep and had few other passengers. He had plenty of money, having sold the three horses he'd taken from the hunting lodge. The ship's master didn't much like the look of Tullo, but he liked the look of his silver, and it was hard and true to the bite, so he pouched it and let the stocky, disagreeable man on board; and his horse, for which, naturally, he charged extra. So by the time Sir Edmund bounced into the English camp on the wretched pack pony, Tullo was sailing away into the twilight.

The ship was too far distant for Brind to see; and he didn't know that the cloud of dust three miles away, kicked up by Sir Richard Baret's troop as it returned to Calais, contained Sir Edmund.

Brind was anxious to press on toward the tents, flags, and glimmering cooking fires, anxious to find the Earl of Arundel, but Aurélie wouldn't budge. She said Glaive was exhausted and should be allowed to rest. Brind thought it strange that Aurélie was prepared to spend the night at the edge of the forest rather than reach warmth and food. In the end, though, he sat down, because he didn't think it was right to leave her. He snuggled close to the already sleeping Glaive and hoped his master would be safe at the roadside where they'd left him.

"I wish you good night and a speedy recovery," smiled the tall knight as his men deposited Sir Edmund outside the Earl of Arundel's tent. The farewell was civil enough but Sir Edmund knew that he'd been dumped: without Brind, he was of no further interest to Sir Richard.

He proved to be of no great interest to the Earl of Arundel either. The earl was genuinely glad that Sir Edmund wasn't dead, but with no dogs, no men, and only one good knee, he was of somewhat limited use. The earl suggested he go home. This should have been music to Sir Edmund's ears, but it wasn't. He made allowances—the earl was irritable because of the never-ending siege—but still he felt discarded. And where was Brind?

Sir Edmund hobbled down to the harbor, half hoping to meet and confront Tullo, but there was no sign of him. And no information either. The surly, suspicious seamen lounging on the quay showed little respect for rank, and none at all for rank without money. Sir Edmund limped back to the English camp none the wiser. Tullo might be on his way to England or he might not. Sir Edmund tried to reassure himself that almost certainly Tullo wasn't; that he was still in France and could be intercepted.

But it wasn't the throbbing pain in Sir Edmund's knee that kept him awake all night; it was the fear that Tullo, who believed his master dead, would not be content with the life of a roaming outlaw.

At dawn, Aurélie forced herself to move. She couldn't face saying good-bye to Brind, so she kissed Glaive on both his warm ears instead. When Brind returned triumphantly from the forest with a handful of the honeycomb he knew she loved, Aurélie had gone. The dog boy looked at Glaive, as if for explanation, but the dog merely thumped his tail in anticipation of breakfast. The honeycomb stuck to Glaive's teeth and Brind laughed at his efforts to remove it.

In one way, Brind felt more comfortable without Aurélie. As a companion she was unpredictable, puzzling, and tiring—unlike Glaive, who sought only to please. But Brind waited an hour in case she returned, and when she didn't, he was disappointed and sad. Glaive licked the dog boy's hand in comfort. Or it may have been to get at the last traces of honey.

When Brind and his mastiff walked into the English siege camp, looking for the black and gold checkers of the Earl of Arundel, nobody paid them the slightest attention. The place was a huge canvas city that had spread around the walled town like a fungus, the only gaps in its growth where water or marsh made erecting tents or shacks impossible. It was bigger than the war camp at Portsmouth, more permanent-looking, but it lacked the war camp's eagerness and expectation: nobody here was going anywhere. That is, not until the stubborn citizens of Calais surrendered, or one of the huge wooden siege engines, laboriously assembled by the English, managed to batter a hole in the town wall. To Brind, there seemed to be more carpenters than soldiers, more chickens than carpenters, and more women than anything.

Also, there were deerhounds. Brind recognized the huntsman walking them on the leash. But by the time he recognized the fluttering silver unicorns above the spacious, well-made tent, it was too late. Sir Richard Baret was barring his path.

"Why, Brind!"

For once, the tall knight did sound surprised, but the sure, amused smile soon reappeared.

"Even more miraculous than your handful of grain."

He peered at the small scar on Brind's forehead.

"Is that all you have to show for drowning in blood and water?"

Sir Richard touched the scar and Glaive growled warningly.

"And a dog left as well."

He regarded the mastiff, as if calculating, then smiled again, with a glance at his men, who were gathering around.

"One out of forty is about the score one would expect from your master."

Brind didn't understand the joke but he sensed disrespect.

"Master good," he said.

"Certainly," agreed Sir Richard. "But I've told him of your unfortunate demise, you see, Brind. He thinks you're dead. And now I don't want you running away again. No more leaping to your doom from the top of a cliff. Agreed?"

And he seized Brind with a sudden, strong hand and threw him into the tent. The grassy floor was flattened and hard and Brind landed heavily. Glaive was at his side in an instant, barking and snarling, ready to launch himself at Brind's attackers, but was just as quickly swamped by a gray-blue wave as the deer-hounds swirled into the tent. Brind could only roll into a trampled ball, hands over his head, as the snapping, yelping, and biting raged around and over him.

Sir Edmund heard the noise. Sudden dog fights were nothing unusual: the dogs in the siege camp were as bored as their masters. But this was different; this was truly savage. And he recognized the deep, defiant hound's voice at the heart of the struggle.

Glaive hadn't fully recovered his strength yet, after all his sufferings, but his heart was as big as ever; bigger than those of all the deerhounds put together, for they'd had the fight bred out of them. They could run like the wind, they could lounge decoratively, they could bring a stag to bay, but they couldn't resist the mastiff. Once their element of surprise was lost, so were they. Glaive bit and ripped and threw them like so many hens trapped in their coop with a fox. Those that could still stand backed to the four corners of the tent, teeth bared, growling, but stared down by the fearless dark eyes. Then

Glaive disappeared in a sudden breeze, or so it briefly seemed to Brind.

A net of fine steel mesh hissed through the air and settled over the dog, turning him in an instant from dominance to impotence. Glaive writhed and scrabbled, but Sir Richard himself drew the cords of the net tight, shrinking it so the mastiff could no longer move at all or even bark, constricted into a frightened, glassy-eyed lump on the floor. The deerhounds refound their courage and bounded forward, threatening and nipping their snared enemy. Sir Richard ordered them back and smiled at Brind, who had got to his feet.

"You see, Brind," said Sir Richard. "Now the dog is mine, too."

"The dog is not yours."

The contradiction came from behind the tall knight. He turned to see Sir Edmund pushing his way roughly through the silver and blue uniforms that crowded the tent doorway.

"And nor is the boy."

Sir Edmund stumped straight over to Brind and

stood resolutely behind him, hands clamped on the boy's shoulders. He glared at Sir Richard, who simply acknowledged him with a polite nod.

"Sir Edmund..I'm glad to see your knee so much improved."

The pain in Sir Edmund's knee was excruciating, but he wasn't going to show it.

"What have you done here?" he demanded, looking at the netted mastiff.

"I have protected my property," replied Sir Richard.

He continued with less restraint than usual, safe in the knowledge that whatever happened now, inside this tent, nobody outside it would ever know.

"Just because your cowardly brute of a dog failed to kill Frenchmen, should he be allowed to run amok and kill Englishmen? Or their hounds?"

He indicated two lifeless gray-blue bodies and others licking their wounds. "The beast is a danger to all and should be dispatched. As for the boy—"

"Brind is still mine," said Sir Edmund. "And will remain so. I will defend him to the death."

The crippled knight spoke coolly, but Brind could feel the trembling fingers digging into his shoulders.

Sir Edmund meant what he said. It was no longer simply a matter of keeping a possession. He knew what was right for Brind, and it wasn't Baret and his deerhounds. It was the kennels at Dowe Manor. It was home. He knew that if only he could get Brind safely there, he himself would have retained at least some honor. He would be able to look his wife in the face, as he was looking the tall knight in the face now.

Sir Richard gave a short laugh.

"To the death? My dear man, I have no intention at all of dying."

And he smiled, clearly pleased with the ambiguity of his reply. Then, without warning, he drew his sword: a light, swift movement, as if picking a flower. The fine point of Italian steel came to rest on Glaive's back, tufted through the tight mesh of the net.

"Sir Edmund, let us finish this matter once and

for all. Dog or boy. The choice is yours. You cannot leave this tent with both."

Cannot? Baret had become blunt as well as confident. Sir Edmund glanced at the uniformed men blocking the doorway. Around twenty of them, all armed. To the death it would have to be, then. Unless he chose, on Baret's terms. To his horror, Sir Edmund began to feel his lofty resolve weakening.

Was death really the best option? Was Brind? If Glaive were left here, Sir Edmund's lifework could never be restored as he'd begun to hope. Because Glaive was the best and the only male left. Without Glaive there would be no mating of the bitches back at home. No litters, no pups, no future for the finest pack of mastiffs in all of England. Sir Edmund could find another male from somewhere, Dorset perhaps, but it wouldn't be the same: the bloodline would be broken. The offspring would be no better than mongrels. Sir Edmund didn't want mongrels. He wanted Glaive. But as he struggled against the thought, a curious change of shape began to occur on the flattened grass in front of him. The steel net began to bulge, then swell, then finally tear, as Glaive, with arching back and straightening legs, gave every last ounce of his strength in a bid to break free.

The sight was transfixing, like watching some monster insect straining to emerge from its cocoon. Except the jaws were not those of an insect. Glaive's growl filled the tent and his teeth flashed like knives as his head broke free. Sir Richard made to stab at the dog with his sword, but as he did so, Brind threw himself at the tall knight and hit him full in the stomach with his head, clinging on with teeth and nails as he and the knight toppled to the ground. The sword fell free and Sir Edmund, moving more quickly than he had in twenty years, picked it up. But Glaive was all the weapon he needed, because the uniformed men fled like rabbits as the dog ran at them.

"Leave!" Sir Edmund shouted once at Brind, and the dog boy scrambled obediently away.

Sir Richard lay sprawled, undignified and

helpless, at Sir Edmund's feet. Sir Edmund looked down at him, then raised the beautifully balanced sword with both hands and, with a roar, plunged it hard into the ground an inch from the tall knight's head. He stood, breathing hard, until he received a blink of acknowledgment, then turned away, leaving the sword where it quivered, and stumbled out of the tent after his brave dog boy and the strongest, finest mastiff in all of France.

Only when the three of them were back beneath the sanctuary of the Earl of Arundel's banners did Sir Edmund remember that the searing agony of his knee made standing impossible.

Aurélie was vaguely aware of the noise of fighting dogs, but it was a long way off and of no interest. All thoughts of Brind and Glaive were banished from her mind. She had slipped back through the English lines easily enough; there were so many women and children in the camp that one more made no difference. Besides, the locust-pig sentries were there to stop people getting out, not in.

The empty space between the English camp and the town walls was more desolate than ever, partly because summer was well past now and partly because there were fewer useless mouths than when Aurélie had left. Some, presumably, had drifted away; others died. The latter possibility made Aurélie's stomach churn: there was no sign of her mother.

Aurélie walked the ground in front of Calais twice in each direction. Close to the walls, the grass was littered with great boulders, which had been hurled from time to time by the English trebuchets, giant catapults that so far had made little impact. Aurélie found a small stone and with it scratched a defiant French insult on each of the boulders as she passed. But she couldn't find her mother.

She recognized none of the faces in the various pathetic huddles of survivors gathered under makeshift shelters, and none of the faces recognized her. When she spoke her mother's name, she was answered invariably with a blank shrug.

Not until evening did Aurélie finally turn toward the spot she had been avoiding all day long: the tiny cemetery where shallow graves had been dug in the soft soil near the marshlands. It was the bleakest corner of the whole unhappy place.

Most of the graves had rough wooden crosses poking from them and a few of the crosses were marked with names. Aurélie hoped she wouldn't find the name she dreaded but somehow knew she would. First, though, she found her grandfather's, and was glad at least that he'd been buried decently. Finally, inevitably, the uncomplaining cross with her mother's name carved on it stood before her.

It was the most recent grave of all, which caused Aurélie such a bitter flash of anger that she almost kicked the cross from the ground. Shocked at her own profanity, she fell to her knees, but it took several minutes to rid herself of the notion that somehow her mother had known that Aurélie was on her way back and had deliberately died before they could be reconciled. When common sense and contrition finally took hold, Aurélie felt she had to sacrifice something. She had never given her mother her heart; the least she could give her now was her most treasured possession: the brooch.

Aurélie buried it in the grave as deeply as she could, so it would be closer to her mother and out of sight of thieves. She kissed the wooden cross with dry lips, then rose swiftly and turned her back on Calais forever.

They had only minutes to catch the tide. Sir Edmund was anxious not to remain in the siege camp another night. He had made an enemy of Sir Richard and knew the tall knight was as dangerous as he was languid. Things happened in war, and in war camps.

Sir Edmund could have appealed to the Earl of Arundel: feudally speaking, Sir Richard owed the earl allegiance just as Sir Edmund did. But what was there to appeal about? A squabble over a kennel boy and a dog? One knight's word against another's? The earl had more important things to think about and already regarded Sir Edmund as a nuisance. No, putting the Channel between themselves and Baret was the sensible option—if only they could find a damned boat willing to take them. Shipmasters seemed to do as they liked, unless they had direct orders from the king, or a huge profit in view. Like the common sailors under their command, they took pleasure in being difficult.

In the end, it was Glaive who secured their passage. The master of a wine ship undertook to put Sir Edmund, Brind, and the dog ashore in England, provided Glaive killed twenty rats during the voyage. If he failed to reach that number, laughed the master, showing a yellow tongue and the remains of equally yellow teeth, the mastiff, boy, and knight would be brought straight back to Calais. The ship's crew also laughed, unpleasantly, but Sir Edmund felt he had little choice. He nodded at Brind, who overcame his fear of the sea sufficiently to help Sir Edmund aboard, and they wedged themselves where they could in the waist of the ship.

Like the hold below, the waist was crammed with wine barrels. Perilously so, to Sir Edmund's mind: the ship lay so low, one could lean over the side and almost touch the water. Not that one would want to touch the filthy, rubbish-filled water of Calais harbor. Glaive, already unsettled by the motion of the vessel, pressed close to Brind, who sat stroking the dog's ears continuously, as much for his own comfort as for Glaive's. Now that they were actually on a ship again, Brind's fear had poured back in and drowned his eagerness for home.

The ship's master was a talkative man. He introduced himself as Captain Claret, which drew further laughs and sniggers from the seamen, at whom he shouted various unintelligible orders in between chatting to the distracted Sir Edmund.

"This ship, my lord, is called *The Gannet*. Which is a seabird," he explained helpfully. "And for good reason, for she will fly you home to England by the shortest route. We shall reach Dover in one bound."

A ship that could both fly and bound seemed encouraging; the holes Sir Edmund thought he could see in the single sail as it was hoisted, less so.

"We're a lucky chance for you, my lord," continued Captain Claret. "We shouldn't be here. Up from Gascony, you see, bound for Southampton, but blown halfway to Norseland by contrary winds. Set fair now, though," he promised confidently. "Dover at dawn."

The sail was snagging before it was fully hoisted on its yard. The crew and their captain seemed to settle for less than perfection and the sail hung crumpled and limp, at a slight angle. And Sir Edmund hadn't imagined the holes in it. Nor the frayed nature of the ropes that held the ship to the quayside. He was on the point of changing his mind and disembarking when one of the ragged seamen leaned across him without a word and untied the closest rope, parting the ship from the safety of dry land.

Then, as the seaman moved away, something sprang from the darkening quayside and landed on Sir Edmund's shoulders. He cried out in surprise, but the creature slid lightly past him and settled beside Brind.

"Move over," said Aurélie to the dog boy. "I'm invading England."

IX

THE GANNET AND THE DRAGON

ullo and his horse walked ashore at Rye. It had been a simple crossing, just a few hours, with a favorable wind. Dowe Manor was a long way off, perhaps two days' ride, but that was fine with Tullo. He was safely in England. The hard part was over. As Tullo rode away, the ship's master told him he was a lucky man to have crossed when he did. There was an almighty storm brewing to the west. Tullo didn't answer. He believed you made your own luck.

✦ ✦ ✦

One dawn later, *The Gannet* was still within sight of Calais. The tide had carried her out during the night, but what little wind there had been had soon died and now she bobbed lethargically, like a half-submerged cooking pot. The sea lay around her as thick and smooth as oil. If the ship sank, she would do so silently, with barely a ripple as the heavy black waters closed over her.

Sir Edmund took consolation in the thought that, if *The Gannet* was going nowhere, nor was any other vessel. Therefore Tullo must be stranded in France. Unless he'd left before them. Sir Edmund struggled stiffly to his feet and hobbled off to find the captain. Surely in the absence of flying and bounding, the ship had oars with which to make some kind of headway?

Aurélie sat with her back steadfastly turned to France. Having sworn never to set eyes on Calais again, she had been mortified to wake with the walls of the town still clearly visible. Now she fixed her eyes on *The Gannet*'s airless sail and, clenching her fists, concentrated all her mental powers on summoning up a breeze that would blow her and the ship far away. From the contortion of her face and the whiteness of her knuckles, Brind thought she must be in pain, and he growled softly and tried to stroke her head. Aurélie started and shook him off with a glare, then moved away, leaving Brind as confused as ever.

But the dog boy was pleased she had come back to him and Glaïve, even though she was still difficult to be with. He was excited at the prospect of showing Aurélie the kennels at Dowe Manor, and the rest of the mastiffs waiting for them there. He pictured them all, dogs, girl, and boy, running for sheer joy through the woods and streams of home.

Secretly, Aurélie was looking forward to these things, too. She told herself that pure impulse had made her leap onto the wine ship when she'd seen Brind and Glaïve onboard; that she had gone to the harbor intent solely on boarding a ship to Gascony, perhaps Spain, anywhere south. England, home of the invading locust pigs, had been out of the question. And yet here she was, willing the enemy's coastline to appear, as if it were the only place on earth that held hope of a future for her. Which, in reality, it was. Aurélie was a penniless French orphan, but Sir Edmund hadn't thrown her overboard the moment she'd landed on him. It had been a promising start. Graciously, Aurélie had decided to give Sir Edmund and England a chance.

"Oars? Oars? *The Gannet* is no rowing boat, my lord, she is a sailing ship."

Captain Claret shook his head, as if the ignorance of landsmen never ceased to sadden and amaze him. Then briefly he became businesslike.

"And the girl will cost you another five rats."

He laughed his yellow laugh and Sir Edmund was assailed by sour wine fumes. The sun had barely risen but the man was drunk.

As if to prove the point, the captain lurched sideways, although the ship was perfectly still.

"Will you join Claret for breakfast?" he continued

amiably, indicating a table inside the tiny deck-house which stood beside the mast. On the table were a tapped barrel and a pewter jug.

"We are paid in wine, you see, my lord. By the merchant. So one day from home we take a little on account."

The pewter jug was large. He filled it to the brim and offered it to Sir Edmund with another gassy smile.

"Seagoing tradition."

Sir Edmund doubted that but declined politely and made his way back to Brind and Glaive. He barely noticed Aurélie as he came to terms with their predicament: they were trapped on a rotting, overloaded ship captained by a drunkard. Up on the afterdeck, the helmsman was slumped asleep across the tiller, and the sky to the west was becoming as black as the sea around them. Drops of rain began to fall, intermittent but large. The heavy sound as they hit the wine barrels reminded Sir Edmund of the crossbow bolts snapping into the shields at Crécy.

✦ ✦ ✦

Tullo munched his leisurely breakfast of bread and beans and watched the storm that was filling the Channel, seemingly sucked along it from the west like black smoke up a chimney. As he watched and ate, Tullo idly wondered what it would be like to drown, and how one got to hell from the bottom of the sea. Did the Devil reach up for you from beneath the seabed? If so, wouldn't the water pour through and douse the flames of hell itself? Some poor wretch on a leaky ship was about to find out, probably. But not Tullo.

He remounted his horse. He was less than a day's ride from Dowe Manor now and his path was lit by a curious dull sunlight that ended at the sea's edge.

Brind also watched the weather changing. Calais had disappeared, hidden not by distance but by a dense shroud of rain that had drifted across it swiftly from the west and now was enclosing the flightless *Gannet*. The sea had turned from black to gray, pitted and whipped by the gathering wind.

Brind and Glaive moved in alarm as a sudden pitching of the deck caused the wine barrels to shift. The barrels were poorly secured, and when a yelled curse from Captain Claret woke the helmsman and brought the rest of the crew shambling on deck, it was clear even to Brind that they, like their master, had breakfasted on the cargo.

The seamen made ineffectual attempts to tie down the barrels, but when the first big wave hit *The Gannet* and a barrel broke completely free, they only scampered out of its way as it trundled across the deck and smashed through a patched-up section of the ship's side. Then they gathered to watch in mock despair as it was lost astern.

As more barrels began careering lethally around the deck, the seamen ceased to be amused and scuttled back beneath the foredeck, closing the hatch behind them. Captain Claret cursed them again, colorfully, then promptly disappeared into the deckhouse and locked the door.

The curtains of rain became icy rods and then,

briefly, hailstones that hammered numbingly on the wretched dog and three humans left marooned in the open. Aurélie became enraged. She had lost one potential benefactor to fire; she had no intention of losing another to tempest. Momentarily, she was scared that she had indeed summoned up the wind, but just as quickly dismissed herself as stupid. Clearly, the storm had been coming, and now that it was upon them, something had to be done.

She hammered on the door of the deckhouse but Captain Claret didn't answer. On one side was a small unglazed window. Stretching on tiptoe, Aurélie could just see through it. She glimpsed the top of the captain's hat. He was sitting on the floor. Aurélie shouted at him to come out and save his ship.

"Only a shower," he replied. "It'll pass." Then he chuckled. "Has the rat hound not started yet? He's mighty big to get among the barrels, y'know, let alone down in the bilge. You'll be on *The Gannet* the rest of your lives, I reckon. Like

Captain Claret. Back and forth, back and forth . . ."

And he laughed, and choked on his wine as the ship rolled and the badly trimmed sail above Aurélie's head slapped madly against the mast. Aurélie cursed the captain with all the rude words she'd ever learned, then fell on the slippery deck as the ship yawed again.

The remaining loose barrels, which had rolled to one end, now gathered themselves and rumbled toward her like a downhill cavalry charge. Aurélie leaped and grabbed at the roof of the deckhouse, drawing her legs up just in time as the barrels rolled past and crashed into the posts of the foredeck. One of the barrels sprang open within its hoops and dark red wine gushed out, joining the ankle-deep slush of rain and seawater and staining Aurélie's feet as she splashed back to her companions.

Above her on the afterdeck, the tiller flailed back and forth, the helmsman having deserted his post and hidden from the storm with the rest of the crew. Aurélie knew from her slightest of experience of fishing trips with her father that the tiller must be secured at all costs. A directionless boat soon turned sideways to the wind and swell. Once that happened, the boat was helpless; one big wave would swamp it.

"We must turn the ship to the wind!" yelled Aurélie.

Sir Edmund was barely mobile but he was heavy and strong. Once he'd been levered up the steps onto the afterdeck and jammed beside the tiller, he leaned his whole weight against it until *The Gannet* began to turn beneath them. She turned as slowly as if she were stuck in horse glue and Aurélie feared the strain on the tiller and the rudder below would break both, but at last the rain and spray were flying straight in their faces.

"Hold her there!" cried Aurélie.

Sir Edmund nodded. It didn't occur to him not to accept orders from a ten-year-old French girl. Survival was all that mattered. He wrapped his arms around the tiller, braced his good leg, and fought to keep the spiking rain in his eyes.

The wind was gale force now, shrieking through the holes in the sail. At any moment the ancient canvas would rip from top to bottom and fly away. They had to get the sail down, so the wind had nothing to tear at.

Aurélie scrambled back to the waist of the ship, clung on, and tried to make sense of the bewildering array of ropes and rigging that stretched away high to the top of the mast. The mast itself seemed to touch the black sky. Aurélie's fingers and brain were becoming useless with intense cold and hunger. She grew angry with herself for failing.

Then she heard Glaive and, looking up, saw that for some reason the dog had scrabbled his way up onto the foredeck and was standing, head to the wind, ears flying, flanks streaked with spray, barking at the elements. His strange defiance inspired Aurélie. She drove herself on and managed to trace one of the sheets, the ropes that held the bottom corners of the sail, then those that led up to the yard, the long horizontal pole from which the sail was suspended. She and Brind would have to work together, one on either side of the ship.

Aurélie looked around for Brind and was astonished to see him dancing about the deck, dodging the rolling barrels and helping them one by one through the splintered gap in the ship's side. Like Glaive, he seemed to have lost all fear of the sea, as if the explosion of the storm had liberated him, blown the dread out of him, and replaced it with a kind of madness.

Aurélie shouted at him, but the wind snatched the words away and only when he looked up could she get his attention. The ship plunged as he made his way toward her, sending him against the afterdeck stairs in a slithering heap, but he actually howled in reckless delight as he scrambled to his feet.

Aurélie showed Brind the ropes she wanted him to loosen and pull. He seemed to understand but was so wild with excitement she doubted he would concentrate when the moment came to lower the sail. Then she slid to the other side of the ship and fumbled with the tangle of rigging there, before waving her arm at Brind. To her relief he pulled the right ropes and she felt the sail above them slacken and begin to drop. Then stick fast.

Peering up, Aurélie could see where the yard had jammed, still high on the mast, trapped by a knot of rope. In a panic, she tugged and strained, but the yard refused to drop further and the sail billowed and flapped and swung, continuing to be the howling wind's ally in its relentless bid to turn *The Gannet* sideways.

Up on the afterdeck, Sir Edmund still fought with the tiller, but his face was gray and set. He was tiring, as he must, and when he could fight no longer *The Gannet* would be turned and rolled over. Aurélie stared up again at the trapped yard and the swaying mast, her head tilted right back. The low clouds sped by giddily and she lost her balance and fell to the deck. She knew she could never climb up there. She had managed trees, eventually, in the ravine, but she froze at the thought of climbing to the sky. Brind was gripping her arm, helping her stand.

"The sail's stuck!" shouted Aurélie, pointing upward. "We have to free it or we'll drown!"

Brind bared his teeth in what was either a snarl or a grin and hauled himself onto the rigging. A section of rope immediately gave way under his feet but he only laughed and swung himself higher and higher. He might have been looking for honeycomb. And still Aurélie could hear Glaive on the foredeck, barking, barking, barking at the storm. Her whole foaming world had gone mad.

Brind loved to be in the topmost branches of a great tree in a gale. The power of the wind thrilled him. And the creaking and roaring and swishing were not so very different from the sensations of a masthead at sea. Brind didn't look down, though. That was the secret.

If anything, it was easier to climb rigging than a tree: there were far more handholds. Higher up the rope was stronger, with fewer frayed and rotten bits, and Brind climbed with an easy rhythm, only stopping and clinging on tight when the ship heeled over and he felt himself hanging out almost horizontally above the sea. That made him laugh. It was all so different from the caged fear and sickness of his first Channel crossing, and the terror of that sudden crash into the water after which Hatton had lost his boot. Here Brind was in his element, in control. He thought of Hatton and heard him chuckle. Brind hoped he'd found a good pair of boots in heaven.

The rigging took Brind to the very top of the mast. The yard and sail were snagged a little way down, but though Brind could see the tangle of knotted rope and rusty nails that were the problem, he couldn't reach them. He descended a few feet and stretched out his hand again. His fingers touched the rope but could gain no leverage. He considered what to do.

On the deck below, Aurélie could hardly bear to watch. High above her, Brind was perched precariously, like a fragile bird unable to fly. She screamed out loud when, without warning, the dog boy let go of the rigging and leaped at the mast, wrapping his legs around it and hugging it tight.

Eventually, when he felt secure, Brind stopped hugging the mast and, still holding tight with legs and feet, used his hands to work close up on the tangled rope. But neither he nor Aurélie was prepared for what happened as the knot was freed.

The biggest wave yet broke over *The Gannet*'s foredeck with a plunging crash, burying the bow of the ship and sweeping Glaive down into the waist. Aurélie too was washed backward and left floundering, an indignity which saved her life as the yard dropped to the deck, one end smashing through the rigging where she had been standing, before it cartwheeled into the sea. Most of the sail was still attached to the yard but caught on board, so that the whole waist of the ship was filled with boiling sea and fallen sail.

To Brind, looking down, it seemed as if a dirty-white cloud had descended from the sky and enveloped the ship beneath him. Looking down. Brind quickly closed his eyes, but it was too late. A cold sweat tingled through him, leaving him shaking, and his stomach rose to his throat. *The*

Gannet's bow also rose, sluggishly, as the mighty wave rolled astern. And as the bow rose, the mast leaned backward, backward, determined to loosen Brind's grip. And he fell.

Aurélie screamed again as Brind plummeted toward her. A scream of loss rather than fear. Then she quickly looked away. But there was no shattering thud to make her flinch and feel sick. For a moment she thought he must have hit the sea rather than the deck, but there had been no splash either, so she risked a look and saw the dog boy rolling and bouncing toward her over the settling sail. Air trapped beneath it had broken his fall and he was laughing. Laughing.

Aurélie tore at Brind in a fury. She felt foolish at having shown she cared so much whether he lived or died, and to have that moment of weakness thrown back at her by his cheerfully *not* dying was too much. Brind fended her off in his usual bewildered way, but as they grappled he had a sudden inspiration: these unprovoked attacks of Aurélie's were really in play; she was just an unpredictable puppy, for whom sudden fighting was a game. Still exhilarated by the storm and his soft landing, Brind laughed still more and fought back, and soon Glaive was struggling toward them through the water, barking jealously at being left out.

A roar of anguish from above brought a stop to the sudden, bizarre tussle. Aurélie broke away and splashed up the steps onto the afterdeck. Sir Edmund was still clutching the tiller but the tiller was no longer attached to the rudder. The exhausted knight held up the tiller hopelessly, then hurled it into the sea. Peering over the stern, Aurélie could see that the rudder itself was broken as well and coming adrift from the sternpost. The strain on the steering gear had taken its toll and Brind's heroics in bringing down the sail had been too late, or, at any rate, in vain. *The Gannet* was beyond their control now. They were at the mercy of the storm.

Already the ship was lurching around, weary of fighting, ready to surrender. Peace on the seabed beckoned her. Sir Edmund instinctively grabbed both Brind and Aurélie and pulled them to him, as if close proximity somehow would provide strength, like a shield wall. Glaive stood in front of them, barking again; daring the mountainous seas to do their worst. The waves were rearing higher still and seemed to pause, considering their moment of attack, before rolling irresistibly forward.

The Gannet rose awkwardly over the next assault, broadside on, but when she slid into the dark trough that followed, a further tower of water was already building above her. Brind glanced down into the waist of the ship to see the now waterlogged sail covered in scurrying black. Rats. Whiffling urgently in search of safety. There were nearer two hundred of them than the twenty-five Glaive was supposed to kill. And then there were none, as the great tower of water tumbled down on *The Gannet*, Sir Edmund's shield wall was swept away and the unconscious Captain Claret, like all worthy captains should, went down with his ship.

✦ ✦ ✦

Brind thought he was being carried to heaven. He thought he must be on the great white cloud he'd looked down on from the mast. The cloud was wet, but then, clouds brought rain, so that was only right. Sir Edmund was close by, on the same cloud. Glaive as well. It pleased Brind to know that dogs went to heaven. And Aurélie was beside him. Brind was glad of that, too. She would meet Hatton. But Aurélie was punching Brind. And shouting at him.

"Stay awake! Stay awake!"

And Brind realized he was not on his way to heaven but drifting in a gray, cold hell of heaving sea and angry, tearing cloud.

Aurélie turned her attention to Sir Edmund, who also was beginning to fade into the cold sleep, his grip on the yard loosening. She pinched his ear as hard as she could and his closing eyes sprang open.

"Hold on, my lord! The storm is passing."

Aurélie's voice was weaker than her spirit.

✦ ✦ ✦

The great wave that had engulfed *The Gannet* had done her passengers a strange favor. It had carried them clear of the sinking ship, so they were not sucked down in the swirling vortex that briefly followed her to the bottom. And it had dragged away the fallen yard and sail, fetching this wreckage up against the three survivors and their dog as they surfaced, coughing seawater and waiting to die. The yard and its sail hadn't come down from the mast in the way Aurélie had intended, but they were their salvation now — at least for as long as they could hold on. They clung in a row to the floating pole, and the sail, spread beneath them like the wing of a ghostly giant ray, provided some support, especially for Glaive, who had no hands with which to grip but had straddled the yard with his front legs. This meant his head and body were raised higher than the others' and gave him the appearance of being in command.

For a while, giant waves continued to swell and hunch over them, shutting out the sky before lifting them high, so that Aurélie thought she could see all the way to England, and then sliding past and dropping them into the next dark valley. But none broke over them. And eventually it was as if the sea became bored with toying with them and hurried on its way in an irritated, choppy fashion, taking what was left of the storm with it. But there was still the cold sleep. Aurélie knew it would kill them all soon. They had to get out of the water.

The long-necked dragon came toward Glaive with fixed eyes. Its open mouth showed a forked red tongue and its horny scales were raised like hackles. The dog bared his teeth and growled, then began to bark, scrabbling vainly with his hind feet to gain a grip on the submerged sail. None of the humans could see the dragon as it dodged between the waves, only Glaive, with his higher vantage point; and though his barking stirred them from their lethargy, it was upon them before Aurélie or Brind or Sir Edmund was aware of it. The dragon hit the yard, then became hampered by the unexpected sail and came to rest, ignoring Glaive's furious attempts to sink his teeth into its neck. It had no mind to strike back and felt no pain.

"A boat!" cried Aurélie.

And either her words or the unpleasant taste of painted wood made Glaive fall back and thrash in the water, as if he'd known all along that the threatening monster wasn't real.

The dragon boat lay heaving above them, its prow bumping and scraping against the yard, but nobody answered Aurélie's feeble calls for help. Nobody even peered over the dragon's shoulder at her. The curved sides of the boat were high and unclimbable, and for a desperate moment Aurélie feared it would plough straight on, leaving them all behind like so much flotsam. But she could see no sail to drive it forward. She called again, and Sir Edmund, stirred to consciousness and realizing there was a chance of rescue, added his own cracked voice. Glaive began to bark again. It was impossible for anyone on board not to hear them.

Toward the stern some strands of rope and

rigging trailed over the dragon boat's side. Aurélie turned to see Brind allowing himself to float free of the yard, pulling Glaive with him. Brind clung tightly to the dog's neck, speaking in his ear, and Glaive paddled gamely toward the stern, his nose just above water. The current pushed against him and, as she watched, Aurélie was filled with a new fear: that having survived the storm, Glaive and Brind would be simply carried away. But Brind started kicking with his feet and slowly dog and boy began to edge back toward the boat.

They missed the rope at the first attempt, but Brind managed to grab it on the second. He lay resting in the water, gathering his strength, then, planting his feet on the slippery planking, hauled himself hand over hand up the side. Glaive, unable to follow, could only bark in frustration and tread water.

Once on deck, Brind found more rope and padded forward to the dragon's neck. The rope snaked down, Aurélie grabbed it, and Brind braced himself against the boat's side while she climbed up. Sir Edmund was much more of a problem. Because of his injured knee, he couldn't climb. He was a dead weight and, even when he managed to tie a rope around his waist, they couldn't lift him.

Despite the fearsome dragon's head, the boat was a modest cargo vessel of the kind that had crisscrossed the Channel since the days of the Conqueror and before. Its sail and mast, like its crew, were gone, broken and carried away by the storm, but among the jumble of broken kegs and waterlogged bales that remained on board Aurélie found what she was looking for: a rope cradle used for loading and unloading, and the pulleys and wooden props that were supposed to operate and support it.

Aurélie spent an hour reconstructing the mechanism, with a patience that surprised Brind, and when they finally lowered the cradle for Sir Edmund and Glaive to struggle into, she held her breath, expecting the whole rig to collapse once it came under strain. But it didn't and, with much creaking of rope on wheel and the occasional heart-stopping jolt, the shivering knight and mastiff were slowly winched up together and swung on board — the strangest catch ever hauled from the deep.

As Glaive shook himself and Sir Edmund lay gratefully on the dry, hard deck, the sun appeared and its brief, blinding rays warmed them all and made them smile. There was even food on the dragon boat. Some of the kegs contained pickled herrings, others heavy, round cheeses as hard and gritty as millstones. The three survivors and their dog were still at the mercy of wind and tide but they were out of the deadly cold sea and they wouldn't starve. The tragic emptiness of the dragon boat didn't greatly affect them. They were alive, and so were their hopes of reaching home.

As the four of them sat together behind the dragon's head, it felt to a suddenly euphoric Sir Edmund as if the dog boy and the intense little French girl, hunched at his feet gnawing cheese, had become his children. He patted Glaive, fed him a herring, and relaxed.

But if Sir Edmund could have seen his fireside rather than simply anticipating it, he would have felt a deep dread as Lady Beatrice opened the door of Dowe Manor and a dark shadow fell across her.

X

FIND HOME

Lady Beatrice walked slowly away from the door, stared out the window, then sat down. Tullo had followed her in, uninvited. He stood by the hearth, glancing around the great hall as if trying it for size, while he waited for his lord's wife to speak.

"How did he die?" she asked at last, quietly.

"Bravely," said Tullo.

The respect and humility in his voice were unfamiliar, but he had practised hard.

"At Crécy? We had news of a great battle. A victory. Did he die there?"

Eventually there would be a list of the knights who had fallen at Crécy. An accurate list. Tullo was prepared to tell certain bits of truth where necessary. "No, my lady. He survived the battle."

"How, then?"

He wanted her to look at him but, as yet, she wouldn't.

"He was captured, by a French knight of rank, to be ransomed. He was considered a fine catch."

Lady Beatrice looked up now, her intelligent eyes fixed on Tullo, as if this last sentence didn't quite ring true. He had to be careful not to overdo the compliments. Sincerity wasn't his greatest strength. Nor was patience; but patience was essential.

"There was a fire," continued Tullo, keeping it simple. "At the French knight's hunting lodge. Both the Frenchman and my master died."

"How do you know this?"

The lady was still looking straight at him, and frowning.

"From Philip, his page, who escaped the fire

but then was left for dead by the routiers who caused it."

"Routiers?"

She didn't understand the term.

"French war bands, my lady. Cutthroats who spit in the face of chivalry. I found the boy before he died of his wounds."

This was the moment. Tullo took the precious folded parchment from his jerkin and, with a sad, respectful bow, presented it to Lady Beatrice.

"Philip was to have delivered this," said Tullo. "My master wrote it before the fire."

He had repaired the seal by softening the wax. He hoped she wouldn't notice. Lady Beatrice didn't accept the letter straightaway. Tullo looked humbly at the floor. Eventually he felt her take the package lightly from his fingers. He didn't realize she had left the room until he heard a door close.

In her chamber, Lady Beatrice barely glanced at the seal as she broke it and unfolded the parchment with trembling fingers. She scanned the letter quickly then sat down before rereading it properly. It was misspelled, rambling, and uncharacteristically sentimental, but undeniably it was written by her husband. If he were dead, the ransom of forty mastiffs was irrelevant. If he were dead, everything was irrelevant.

Lady Beatrice mechanically refolded the letter, her hands no longer shaking, and gazed at the cold, blank wall for a long time. If required to write down her husband's faults, she would have needed a larger sheet of parchment than she was clutching now, but cruelty and arrogance had not been among them. At heart, he had been a kind man and she had loved him for it. She had been a far luckier wife than most. Lady Beatrice held the letter tighter and allowed herself to grieve.

Tullo had not felt it necessary to stare humbly at the floor for very long. He straightened up after the door closed and resumed his visual inventory of the hall. The lady hadn't dismissed him before leaving with the letter, so he thought it was proper enough for him to remain.

The hall was not unfamiliar. The manor servants were entertained in it twice a year, at Christmas and harvest. It was a good size, but not grandiose. A good oak board, a few faded hangings. Comfortable, old-fashioned, no proper chimney. Smoky when the firewood was damp.

Tullo couldn't help becoming a little tense. Giving Lady Beatrice the letter had been a gamble. It proved Sir Edmund had been a prisoner; it didn't prove he was dead. She had only Tullo's word for that. But the vital thing was that Tullo knew he *was* dead. No matter how doubtful or reluctant Lady Beatrice remained, no matter how long she waited, her husband would never again ride into the yard at Dowe Manor. She herself was no longer a young maid. There were few men of rank who would consider the widow of Dowe a worthwhile prospect, and fewer still every day the war continued. Kempe, the neighbor, was old and feeble and could be kept at arm's length with no trouble.

Tullo sat on a carved chair. He had never sat on a chair in this hall before, only on the bench. He didn't have marriage in mind; the gulf in rank between himself and Lady Beatrice was too deep and wide to be imagined, let alone bridged. But, eventually, she would need a man. Somebody who knew how to run a manor farm and its lands. A protector for herself and a steward for her property. And stewards didn't live in hovels like huntsmen did. Stewards lived in comfort. Stewards had control. Tullo wanted nothing more than that. And nothing less.

Lady Beatrice paused and composed herself. She heard a swift movement as she opened the door, but as she went into the hall Tullo was standing as she had left him, a picture of condolence and humility. She wondered what he was really thinking.

"I thank you for your good service in bringing me the letter," she said. "Is there news of Hatton?"

"Killed at Crécy, my lady."

She looked sad, as if the idiot carter's death mattered to her.

"And Brind?" she asked, after a pause.

"Also dead."

Lady Beatrice turned away. Tullo exulted inwardly. She hadn't challenged him further on Sir Edmund's fate. There was an air of acceptance about her. At length he spoke to her stiff, upright back.

"Shall I tend the dogs, my lady?"

"Yes, Tullo," she said. "You may tend the dogs."

The fishermen were English but dangerous. The dragon boat without mast or steering oar was a prize and only the growling presence of Glaive dissuaded them from tipping its occupants into the sea when they swarmed on board to claim it. They rootled through the damaged cargo, argued among themselves as to whether to unload the goods onto their own craft or take the dragon boat in tow, finally decided on the latter, and a day later had dragged it onto the shingle beach below their poor, stinking village.

Once its deck had been picked clean and every last herring, cheese, bale of wool, and bowstave squirreled away in the nearby hovels, the dragon boat itself was hauled high above the tide line, ready to be stripped of its timbers, or, better still, sold back to its owner, should that unfortunate merchant ever learn of its whereabouts.

Sir Edmund, Brind, and Aurélie were completely ignored as the excited villagers dashed back and forth, obsessed with their treasure trove. Sir Edmund politely asked, then loudly demanded, the name of the place where they'd landed but nobody answered, so in the end the three unwanted strangers and their dog trudged away.

Aurélie thought it a strange welcome to her new country, and, as they passed through the deserted village, was all for "borrowing" a tethered donkey that they came across, as recompense for the villagers' lack of respect and hospitality. But Sir Edmund, still stung by the memory of his ride on Sir Richard Baret's pack pony, said no—forcefully. He would crawl home if necessary. Wherever home was.

However, on the inland edge of the village they passed a great heap of driftwood, piled there for some future purpose, and Brind dragged from it a bleached tree branch, forked at just the right height to fit under Sir Edmund's arm. When he offered the crutch to Sir Edmund, the knight accepted, which annoyed Aurélie, as if she and Brind were rivals for Sir Edmund's patronage and she'd been passed over unfairly. Now that she actually was in England, she'd begun to worry again.

Sir Edmund worried, too, about Aurélie. It had been all very well to think of her, during the two days and nights of danger at sea, as a daughter, but the plain fact was she was no such thing. What was Beatrice going to say? Would she be pleased to be presented with a ready-grown child or insulted? And what if Aurélie proved to be a nuisance? She had the potential for that. What could they do with her then? It would be difficult to dismiss a girl, French or otherwise, who had saved one's life. Twice.

They made their way farther inland and uphill, in the hope that if they climbed the downs some landmark would become visible that Sir Edmund recognized, but none did. So they had to make a choice: turn west or east. Glaive, however, was in no doubt at all. He stood with his head raised, letting the downland breeze float across his senses, then looked expectantly at Brind.

"Find home," said the dog boy, and Glaive was off, bounding west across the short, springy turf. And with a howl of delight and certainty, Brind raced after him, then stopped abruptly and hurried back to Sir Edmund.

"Go on, boy, go on. Run!" cried the crippled knight, impatiently waving his tree branch.

So Brind ran. And Glaive circled around and leaped at him, and boy and dog tumbled on the grass, barking and laughing.

Aurélie walked demurely beside Sir Edmund. She wasn't irritated by yet more finding—she wanted Glaive to find home more than she wanted anything. Once she got to Dowe Manor, she told herself fervently, all would be well.

Tullo had been right about neighbor Kempe: he proved easy to frighten off. Not that Tullo was explicitly threatening. He just let the old man know that neither Lady Beatrice nor the mastiffs needed his attention now their huntsman was back. Kempe had always been wary of Tullo and, in truth, was not unhappy to relinquish his responsibility for Lady Beatrice. Winter was coming on and the ride from his decaying but comfortable hall across to Dowe was a long and cold one. Rheumatism made it difficult for him to climb on a horse even now. He required Tullo to offer his condolences to Lady Beatrice on the loss of her husband and asked to be informed if Sir Edmund's death were to be marked in a religious way. Not having been educated by priests, he himself was unsure whether there could be a funeral without a body, but no doubt minds better than his would resolve that difficulty. If he were able, he would attend.

Tullo patiently allowed the old man to waffle his conscience to sleep; then, having no conscience of his own, he rode away, smirking at the weakness of his supposed betters.

Lady Beatrice felt a slight chill when Tullo informed her that Kempe would not be coming to Dowe again. Without Kempe, she was isolated. Her only other neighbor, far distant, was her husband's liege lord, the Earl of Arundel. And he was in France. Dowe was a forgotten place. Lady Beatrice sat alone in her chamber, listening to Tullo in the kennels using his whip on the female mastiffs, and the chill grew stronger.

In the days that followed, the sense of menace continued to increase. Tullo lingered longer in the hall when reporting on farm and forest matters. He tethered his horse in his former master's stable. He began to eat his meals in the kitchen. Wherever Lady Beatrice was, she seemed to be able to see or hear him. He never overstepped the mark.

Or never quite enough for her to reprimand him. But, when he made sure she could overhear his conversation with Milda, the kitchen girl, in which he talked of going off to war again, Lady Beatrice knew she was being nudged toward acknowledging him as indispensable. The war had led to a chronic shortage of able-bodied men and already this year's harvest had been mostly lost.

Lady Beatrice, like Tullo, was well aware that, if he left, the manor would sink. She wanted to call his bluff and send him packing, but although she was a brave and proud woman, she shied away from doing so. There were the remaining servants to consider: Milda and the few laborers and their wives. She couldn't abandon them. Nor could she abandon the manor itself: it was her husband's. Lady Beatrice had no children to leave it to, but, for Sir Edmund's sake, she must preserve and nurture it for as long as she could. Which meant accepting Tullo, and the daily nibbling away of her authority. In any case, if she ordered him to leave, would he actually go?

It was a frightening question but it had to be faced, and Lady Beatrice had already begun to doubt the answer. She went to her husband's war chest, found a rusty dagger, and slept with it under her pillow.

They climbed through a beech wood, carpeted with the gold of autumn, and emerged onto another ridge. Along the ridge ran a familiar track, rutted in the chalk. The ruts made Sir Edmund think of Hatton, plodding along with his cart in previous autumns, and of how that simple, earthbound man's heart would have leaped now in recognition that home was just a forested hill away. It was a bittersweet thought, overwhelming Sir Edmund's relief that a week's painful walking from the coast was over, but he brushed it away when he heard hound music.

As if in welcome, the music called from far off in the forest and was coming closer. Brind and Glaive heard it, too, and both stopped, poised, listening intently to the voices they remembered so well.

When the mastiffs finally appeared, a dark wedge in the valley below, Glaive whined and trembled and looked at Brind in hope of the word that would release him to hurtle down the hill and rejoin his pack. But before Brind could give it, Sir Edmund stopped him. Glancing up at his master, Brind saw that the relief and joy of homecoming had disappeared.

The knight was still gazing at the mastiffs as they turned across the valley and disappeared back into the trees, but his face was tense and grim. Brind hadn't recognized the distant horseman with the pack. Or heard his whip. But Sir Edmund had.

Back at the kennels after the hunt, which had been unsuccessful, Tullo strode among the steaming mastiffs as they milled and jostled in their paddock, eager to push their way into the feeding yard. He cracked his whip at the overboisterous members of the pack and kicked those who were too quiet. No natural leader of the bitches had emerged in the long months of separation from Glaive and the other half of the pack, but every one of them remembered the huntsman's whip and boot. They hung close together now for mutual protection. In Tullo's view they'd gone to ruin in his absence. They were barely worth reforming, but that wouldn't stop him from trying. Punishment was the remedy for their slackness and bad habits, and nobody punished like Tullo.

As he watched the mastiffs gobble their supper, Tullo began to think of his own, and of Lady Beatrice eating hers so delicately. He wondered if the time had come to suggest he eat in the hall. Perhaps if he arrived as Milda was about to serve, the lady herself might invite him. After all, there was much to discuss about the future of the manor, and what better time to talk than over supper?

When the last mastiff had eaten, Tullo decided not to let the pack into their sleeping lodge. They'd been too lazy today to deserve sleep. They could stay in their paddock until he was good and ready.

He shut the gate firmly, turned toward the hall, and stopped.

If Tullo had a heart, it missed several beats. For the dead stood before him. Glaive, the French girl, the little cur. And the old fool himself. His master.

Tullo gazed at each in turn, stunned; then became half fearful, half hopeful that they would shimmer and fade, that they were only ghosts come to haunt him. But none of them faded. And the twisted white branch on which Sir Edmund leaned was real enough: its end had left a trail of small dark holes across the mud of the yard.

Tullo wondered why nobody spoke. Why Sir Edmund didn't challenge him about Philip's death. Most of all he wondered how they had survived the fire. It was impossible. But he fell to his knees with the best show of happiness he could manage.

"Master! Thanks be to heaven that you're safe!"

Something smashed on the ground in front of him, thrown by Sir Edmund, and Tullo flinched at the unexpected violence. Then, looking down at the shards, he recognized the blackened neck and small curved handle of the earthenware pot. His mind began to work now.

He was still holding his whip, coiled and ready to hurt. It would give him a chance. He was glad he hadn't stabled his horse. Instead, it was still tethered outside the kennels. He had only to jump the fence behind him, cross the small paddock, and he was free. Mount and ride like the wind. They'd never catch him. Never find him. Not even with Glaive.

Tullo picked up a piece of the earthenware with his free hand and slowly stood up, examining it thoughtfully. He looked at Sir Edmund with a small, cold smile and shrugged, as if acknowledging defeat. Then he hurled the jagged shard with all his strength and malice at Sir Edmund's head, turned, and vaulted the fence.

Sir Edmund was slow to dodge and the shard struck him above the ear. He fell with blood already flowing from the wound, and Aurélie cried out and knelt beside him. But Brind barked a command at Glaive and the great mastiff launched himself at the fence, clearing it cleanly and landing among the excited dogs beyond. Already Tullo was wading swiftly through them, lashing out with his whip; but, with a growl that came from the depths of his soul, Glaive charged after him and the rest of the pack responded to the return of their leader. As one, they surged toward Tullo and mobbed him as he reached the far fence.

He was inches from his horse, inches from escape, as Glaive's teeth sank into his leg and hauled him down. The whip that had caused so much pain and fear fell useless among the churning, snarling bodies, and Tullo followed it under. His last glimpse of life was of the pale evening sky, and of the little cur, standing on the paddock fence. The dog boy. Always the dog boy. Tullo died as he had lived, filled with anger, spite, and jealousy. Brind was shouting but Tullo couldn't hear him. Nor did the dogs.

Brind knew what was happening to Tullo but he felt no sense of the justice of it: that the cruel man who had tried to kill him more than once was now himself being killed. The dog boy's moment of vengefulness, on the night after Crécy, had given him no taste for more. But for the first time in his life among the mastiffs, his voice was now ignored. And so was his magic grain.

Lady Beatrice couldn't stop weeping. No matter how she chastised herself and pulled herself together, she couldn't stop. Milda was just as bad. In the end, Sir Edmund shooed Aurélie and Brind away and shut the door on them, but Aurélie glimpsed the knight and his wife embracing as the door closed. She considered the weeping and embracing a very good sign. Clearly the lady was no dried-up old fish-face who would coldly send her on her way. Nevertheless, she fretted outside the hall, straining to hear what was being said, though the voices were too quiet and private; and waited, shaking her head at Milda's invitation to come and eat in the kitchen.

Brind went willingly enough with Milda, though he was no longer hungry. Home seemed unreal, and Tullo's death, still frighteningly vivid before him, no cause for celebration. He wanted to be in his kennel but couldn't bear to go there. Not tonight.

After a while, the dog boy left the kitchen and took himself off to the same corner of the old stable where he'd first been found twelve summers ago; and there he curled up and let the fussing and grumbling of the hens fill his head and eventually send him to sleep.

As she took a breath and opened the door of the great hall, Lady Beatrice was reminded of the moment, similarly tearstained, when she'd opened the same door just over a week ago, after having grieved the loss of her husband. Then, inside the door, had been the disquieting Tullo. Now, outside it, stood a thin, nervous child.

"Come in," said Lady Beatrice, in what she hoped was a welcoming voice.

Aurélie followed the lady in and closed the door politely behind them. Sir Edmund was sitting by the fire. The lady sat down opposite him and beckoned Aurélie toward them. Aurélie came close to the fire before giving them both her best curtsy. Her knees shook.

Lady Beatrice studied the girl closely, gauging her against what she'd been told already by Sir Edmund. Clearly, despite the curtsy, Aurélie was no aristocrat; but, from what little Lady Beatrice had seen so far, her manners were good, and, apparently, she could read and write. These things mattered, but not as much to Lady Beatrice as character. She didn't want a child she couldn't trust.

"Look at me, Aurélie." She spoke in her usual Norman French.

The girl did as she was asked. She didn't look a happy child. Small wonder. And that could be changed, of course. Determined, even fierce. Yet vulnerable. A child who tried too hard, perhaps. But was she honest? Probably. If dealt with honestly.

Lady Beatrice told herself to stop such wishful guesswork. Was there something in the girl that could be helped and worked on or was there not? Would she be worth the effort? Lady Beatrice hesitated, then made up her mind.

"My husband says he has brought me a daughter all the way from France." She was rewarded with a relieved smile that transformed the hard little face, and a courteous reply in the mother tongue that she and the young girl shared.

"Your husband is too kind, my lady. I hope I shall be worthy of the honor."

That night, for the first time since she had become a useless mouth in Calais, Aurélie slept in a bed. The chamber she had been shown to was small and bare. The walls weren't straight and she could hear mice within them. But there was a window and there was fragrant dried lavender in a bowl on a small table. It was to be her room. A daughter's room. She wanted to be awake when the sun's first rays lit the window. To be lying there safe and secure and feeling the sun warming her. But she fell asleep just before dawn and missed the moment. And when she did wake, her first thought was of Brind.

Sir Edmund had been up since long before dawn. He wanted it finished before the fresh new day. The final act of a dark time. The digging was difficult but his determination gave him strength. That and his thankfulness that it was all over.

Tullo's body had disappeared deep beneath the loam and the grave was almost filled when Sir Edmund looked up to find Brind standing, watching. Sir Edmund held the spade toward him, but the dog boy shook his head sharply and backed away. Sir Edmund said nothing, just continued shoveling soil until the ground was level, then flattened it firmly. He had dug the grave at the edge of the forest, where the brambles would take hold quickly and cover it. Tullo's body would rest undisturbed. His soul wasn't Sir Edmund's concern.

The knight threw down the spade and moved stiffly toward Brind.

Eventually, the dog boy looked away from the

freshly turned earth. "Glaive not obey," he said, and the strange growling voice was unhappy.

Brind, who had suffered most at Tullo's hands, was the only one stricken by his death. Sir Edmund put an arm around the dog boy's shoulder and led him back toward the manor and the growing sunshine.

They stopped by the kennels. The female mastiffs were awake inside their sleeping lodge, noisily restless. Alone in the male quarters, Glaive, too, was giving voice. Sir Edmund had been thinking hard of what to say to Brind. Tullo was gone; he didn't want his shadow to remain. He looked down at the dog boy.

"Tullo was the enemy of the pack," he said. "Glaive did what was right." He paused. "Glaive did what was right, Brind. He is pack leader." Then he squeezed Brind's shoulder before concluding, "And you are my new huntsman."

The dog boy looked up in surprise, and Sir Edmund could see the shadow lifting.

"So exercise the dogs, please," he said gruffly.

"And look after Glaive. I shall soon be requiring him to take a wife."

And he limped off to find some breakfast. His new daughter met him on his way across the yard and he grunted her a good morning as he passed.

Brind ducked into the sleeping lodge but went no further. On the bench, Glaive sat up but hesitated, his tail moving only slowly as he looked uncertainly toward the dog boy. There had been no approval after the huntsman's death. The boy had kept himself separate. And now he was merely crouching in the dark doorway, with no word of greeting, no gesture of command.

Then at last, Glaive whimpered softly and began to crawl forward, and as he did so Brind suddenly fell on him and hugged him tight, and Glaive lapped at the salt around the boy's eyes until the tears had ceased and dog and boy were as one again. Inseparable.

Glaive found himself with three wives eventually—Sallet, Gambeson, and Jupon—but not until the following spring, because that was the best time for the mastiffs to mate, so that the whelps would be born in May and grow with the summer sun to warm and strengthen them.

By the time of mating, Glaive had fully recovered his own weight and strength. He would have his scar forever, but it gradually faded to a white line through his coat, a marking rather than an obvious injury. He proved more interested in mating than in fatherhood, but that was the way of things. He wasn't welcome in the whelping boxes, where the new mothers fed and licked their young constantly and protected them from all comers, father included. Even Brind kept his distance for the first few weeks, before introducing the pups to the wide world outside. And for a few weeks after that he spent most of his time retrieving various favored pups from Aurélie's room, where she tried to keep them as secret pets.

Sir Edmund left Brind to it. The females had never looked in better, more shining health; half the newborns were male; and all survived.

The finest pack of mastiffs in all of England was being rebuilt and, in Brind's instinctive care, would flourish.

The tall knight leaned forward in his saddle and listened. Now he could hear only the whispering of the wind in the grass. He liked the sound. It had been well over two years since he'd heard it. And the smell, too.

In France the wind had in it always the smell of burned thatch. Here on the English downs, even in autumn, it was fresh and sweet. He had not imagined the voices either. Straight ahead. He urged his horse on and his men-at-arms followed, harnesses chinking as they trotted toward the brow of the hill. And then the sound grew in a crescendo as the dogs appeared: sixty mastiffs, old and young in full stride and full voice. They surged past the tall knight as if he and his men were a clump of stunted trees.

The tall knight glimpsed a streak of white on the pack leader's flank as the dogs went by and he braced himself for who might follow. Three horses. The girl on one. Grown a little in two years, but not much. The dog boy. And finally Sir Edmund. The dog boy rode well, almost as easy with a horse as he was with dogs.

"Good day, Brind," called Sir Richard.

He smiled as the dog boy reined in his horse and returned the look warily. Sir Edmund had drawn alongside Brind. He didn't smile either, which Sir Richard thought a shame.

"Sir Edmund, it is good to see you. And the fine young lady," he added, with the familiar nod of mock courtesy.

Sir Richard rode closer but motioned his men to stay where they were. His horse was taller than Sir Edmund's and looked down on it. He smiled again at Sir Edmund, who hadn't returned his greeting. Then the tall knight swiftly drew his sword. The sudden movement frightened Sir Edmund's horse and it shied away. Sir Edmund clung on and righted himself, ready to fight, except he had no weapon other than the hunting bow slung across his back. But Sir Richard simply laughed and tossed the sword in the air, deftly caught its blade in his gloved hand as it fell, then held its hilt toward Sir Edmund.

"You left this in my tent at Calais," he said. "When I yielded. Please take it now. The debt has bothered me."

Sir Edmund was astonished, but still watchful.

"There is no debt," he said.

"Then take it in friendship."

The tall knight held the sword hilt closer. Sir Edmund felt he had no choice. He took the sword.

"Good." Sir Richard smiled, sitting back in his saddle and glancing at Brind. "Now that we are friends again, perhaps we shall hunt together."

Sir Edmund slipped the sword through his belt. He was imagining how it would look on the now empty wall above his war chest. A permanent proof of the one moment in his life he could be truly proud of: when he had risked death to stand by Brind. He looked straight at the tall knight.

"Perhaps we shall," he said. "But perhaps not."

And he spurred his horse forward past Sir Richard and through the men-at-arms, as nobly, Sir Edmund thought, as if he were the king himself. Brind and Aurélie followed and, as they galloped away, the turf flying from their horses' hooves, Brind threw back his head and called, and the now-distant hounds answered and began to turn.

Down into the valley Brind led them, down into the oak woods, where he leaped from his horse and splashed barefoot through the stream.

"Find home!" he cried to Glaive as the dog overtook him. "Find home!"

And Glaive bounded on through the splintered sunlight of the trees, and Brind grasped Aurélie's hand and ran after him, laughing.